A TEXT BOOK OF

ELECTRICAL ENGINEERING MATERIALS
AND
ENERGY CONVERSION

FOR

Semester – III
Second Year Degree Course in
Electrical Engineering

As Per New Revised Syllabus of Shivaji University, Kolhapur
(Effective from 2014)

Miss. PRACHI. R. GODBOLE

M. E. (Electrical)

Mrs. LEENA. N. SURANGLIKAR

M.E. (Electrical)

NIRALI
PRAKASHAN
ADVANCEMENT OF KNOWLEDGE

N2226

ELECTRICAL ENGG. M & E. C. (SEM. III. S.E. ELEC.)   ISBN - 978-93-5164-331-9

First Edition : October 2014

Published By :

NIRALI PRAKASHAN

Abhyudaya Pragati, 1312, Shivaji Nagar,
Off J.M. Road, PUNE – 411005
Tel – (020) 25512336/37/39, Fax – (020) 25511379
Email : niralipune@pragationline.com

DISTRIBUTION CENTRES

PUNE

Nirali Prakashan
119, Budhwar Peth, Jogeshwari Mandir Lane
Pune 411002, Maharashtra
Tel : (020) 2445 2044, 66022708, Fax : (020) 2445 1538
Email : bookorder@pragationline.com

Nirali Prakashan
S. No. 28/25, Dhyari,
Near Pari Company, Pune 411041
Tel : (022) 24690204 Fax : (020) 24690316
Email : dhyari@pragationline.com
bookorder@pragationline.com

MUMBAI

Nirali Prakashan
385, S.V.P. Road, Rasdhara Co-op. Hsg. Society Ltd.,
Girgaum, Mumbai 400004, Maharashtra
Tel : (022) 2385 6339 / 2386 9976, Fax : (022) 2386 9976
Email : niralimumbai@pragationline.com

DISTRIBUTION BRANCHES

NAGPUR
Pratibha Book Distributors
Above Maratha Mandir, Shop No. 3, First Floor,
Rani Jhanshi Square, Sitabuldi, Nagpur 440012,
Maharashtra, Tel : (0712) 254 7129

JALGAON
Nirali Prakashan
34, V. V. Golani Market, Navi Peth, Jalgaon 425001,
Maharashtra, Tel : (0257) 222 0395
Mob : 94234 91860

BENGALURU
Pragati Book House
House No. 1, Sanjeevappa Lane, Avenue Road Cross,
Opp. Rice Church, Bengaluru - 560002.
Tel : (080) 64513344, 64513355,
Mob : 9880582331, 9845021552
Email:bharatsavla@yahoo.com

KOLHAPUR
Nirali Prakashan
New Mahadvar Road,
Kedar Plaza, 1st Floor Opp. IDBI Bank
Kolhapur 416 012, Maharashtra. Mob : 9855046155

CHENNAI

Pragati Books
9/1, Montieth Road, Behind Taas Mahal, Egmore,
Chennai 600008 Tamil Nadu, Tel : (044) 6518 3535,
Mob : 94440 01782 / 98450 21552 / 98805 82331, Email : bharatsavla@yahoo.com

RETAIL OUTLETS

PUNE

Pragati Book Centre
157, Budhwar Peth, Opp. Ratan Talkies,
Pune 411002, Maharashtra
Tel : (020) 2445 8887 / 6602 2707, Fax : (020) 2445 8887

Pragati Book Centre
Amber Chamber, 28/A, Budhwar Peth,
Appa Balwant Chowk, Pune - 411002, Maharashtra,
Tel : (020) 20240335 / 66281669
Email : pbcpune@pragationline.com

Pragati Book Centre
676/B, Budhwar Peth, Opp. Jogeshwari Mandir,
Pune 411002, Maharashtra
Tel : (020) 6601 7784 / 6602 0855

PBC Book Sellers & Stationers
152, Budhwar Peth, Pune 411002, Maharashtra
Tel : (020) 2445 2254 / 6609 2463

MUMBAI

Pragati Book Corner
Indira Niwas, 111 – A, Bhavani Shankar Road, Dadar (W), Mumbai 400028, Maharashtra
Tel : (022) 2422 3526 / 6662 5254, Email : pbcmumbai@pragationline.com

www.pragationline.com   info@pragationline.com

PREFACE

The book is written mainly for the Second Year Students of Electrical Engineering Course for the Subject **"Electrical Engineering Materials and Energy Conversion"**. It is written as per the New Revised Syllabus (2014) of Shivaji University, Kolhapur.

New text book is written, taking in to account all the new features that have been introduced. All the entrants to the engineering field will definitely find this book, complete in all respect. Students will find the subject matter presentation quite lucid. There are large number of illustrative examples and well graded Questions.

Salient features of this book are :

- **Written strictly according to Revised Syllabus of Shivaji University.**
- **Adequate Emphasis on both Theory and Problems.**

Our sincere hope is that the material presented in the book will be useful in understanding the subject as well as for attempting examination questions.

We take this opportunity to express our thanks to **Shri. Dineshbhai Furia** and **Shri. Jignesh Furia** and **Shri. M.P. Munde** for publishing this book in time.

We are also take this opportunity to express our thank all the staff members of Nirali Prakashan Pune namely Mrs. Ulka Chavan, Mrs. Pratibha Bele and also Miss Mandakini for their tremendous dedication and hard work in bringing out this book in an excellent form.

We are also thankful to **Mr. Virdhaval Shinde**, Branch Manager, Kolhapur Office and **Mr. Ashok Nanaware**, Branch Manager, Sangli District for their valuable help and efforts for promotion of our book.

Our special thanks to our family members, students and all those who directly or indirectly supported us in this project.

Any suggestions and feedback shall be appreciated and acknowledged.

October 2014   **Authors**

Pune

SYLLABUS

Unit 1 Conductive Materials   07

General properties and specifications of conductor materials; free electron theory of Metals, Relaxation time, collision time and mean free path, joule's law, factors affecting resistively. Thermal conductivity of metals-Wiedemann Franz law, Properties of high conductive materials (Copper, Brass, Bronzes, and Aluminum), Conductor-bimetals: solders, Materials of high resistively; alloys for use in electrical resistance, precision electrical measuring instruments, arc lamps and electric furnaces. Different types of fuses, fusing current and fuse ratings, materials used for highly loaded metal contacts. Electrical carbon materials: characteristics of different carbon brushes and graphite brushes, Superconductivity.

Unit 2 Insulating Materials   05

General properties of insulating materials (structure, composition). Dielectric gases. Liquid insulating materials. Solid insulating materials, insulating materials for electrical devices. Insulation measurement (Electric strength of liquid) Thermal classification of insulating material.

Unit 3 Magnetic Materials   07

Magnetic parameters (Permeability, magnetic susceptibility, Magnetic moment, Magnetization,). Classification of magnetic materials, Ferromagnetic behavior below critical Temperature, Spontaneous Magnetism and Weiss Theory of Ferromagnetism, Ferromagnetic Materials at high temperature, Ferromagnetic material, Magnetic materials for electrical devices, Soft magnetic materials, Hard magnetic material.

Unit 4 Dielectrics   06

Different types of dielectric materials and their classification, dielectric as an electric field medium. Dielectric properties of insulators in static fields: Dielectric parameters, mechanism of polarization, ionic polarization, orientational polarization, internal field in solids and liquids, , Dielectric losses,

Unit 5 Principles of Electro-Mechanical Energy Conversion   10

Introduction, Flow of Energy in Electromechanical Devices, Energy in magnetic systems (defining energy & Co-energy), Singly Excited Systems; determination of mechanical force, mechanical energy, torque equation , Doubly excited Systems; Energy stored in magnetic field, electromagnetic torque, Generated emf in machines; torque in machines with cylindrical air gap

Unit 6 Materials for Direct Energy Conversion Devices   07

Solar cells, MHD generations, Fuel cells, thermoelectric generator, Thermo ionic converters.

CONTENTS

✠ ✠ ✠

CONDUCTIVE MATERIALS

1.1 INTRODUCTION TO ELECTRICAL CONDUCTING MATERIALS

Depending on current carrying ability of materials they are classified into three general types

- Conductors
- Insulators
- Semiconductors

There are various conducting materials used in electrical engineering. Some of them along with their properties and applications are discussed below.

Properties of Conductors

Electrical Properties

- Resistivity is low.
- Temperature resistance ratio is low.
- Energy dissipated in the form of heat is low.
- Conductivity is good.

Mechanical Properties

- Easy to fabricate.
- Withstand stress and strain.
- Elasticity should be high.
- It must be have high resistance to corrosion.
- It must have solder ability.
- It has good ductility property.

Economical Factors

- Easily available.
- Easy to manufacture.
- Low cost.

1.1.1 Copper

It is reddish brown in colour having the following properties

- High electrical and thermal conductivity. It is highly sensitive towards impurities.
- Its resistance changes with temperature i.e. temperature coefficient of resistance is large.

- As compared to aluminium, copper is having superior heat dissipation capacity.
- Excellent soldering and welding property.
- High tensile strength varies from 3 – 4.8 tonnes/cm^2.
- Its melting point is near about 1100°C.
- Specific gravity is 8.9.
- Its electrical resistivity is 1.682 µΩ cm at 20°C.
- Boiling point is nearly 2600°C.
- It easily forms alloys like bronze, brass etc.
- Temperature coefficient of resistance is 0.00412 per degree centigrade.
- It is malleable and ductile.
- It has high current density.
- Moderate to high strength and hardness.
- Internal conductivity is 397.

Applications

- As its resistance is low, it is more suitable for making electrical wires, cables, making windings of machines and transformer etc.
- It is used for making electromagnets and printed circuit boards.
- It is used for making electrical relays, bus bars and switches.

1.1.2 Aluminium

It is having the following properties

- Poor soldering and welding ability.
- Specific gravity is 2.669
- Its melting point is 660°C.
- Its electrical resistivity is 2.669 µΩ cm at 20°C.
- Boiling point is nearly 1820°C.
- Temperature coefficient of resistance is 0.00412.
- Due to brittleness it can not be twisted.
- Aluminium has most excellent corrosion resistance ability.
- Its resistance is less but large than copper.
- Aluminium is a good electrical and thermal conductor but mechanical strength is less.

- It offers high resistance to corrosion.
- It is ductile and malleable.
- Tensile strength is 9 tones/in^2.
- Easily rolled drawn and forged and it is very soft.
- Welding of aluminium is much more difficult than that of other materials.

Applications

- Powdered aluminium is used in paints, solid rocket fuels.
- It is used for street lighting poles.
- Super purity aluminium can be used in CDS, electronic kits, transistors.
- Used in over head transmission and distribution lines, for bus-bars, for ACSR conductors.
- Aluminium alloys can be used in as an additive to jet fuels, for laser production.
- Wide range household items.
- Used as wires for motors and electrolytic capacitors.

1.1.3 Constantan/Eureka

It is an alloy of copper and nickel. In which 60% copper and 40% nickel is present. It is silver white in appearance. Constantan is having good fatigue life and relatively high elongation capability.

Properties

- It does not rust due to high working temperature.
- Very stable at high working temperature.
- It is having large temperature coefficient of resistance.
- Tensile strength is nearly 52 kg/mm^2.
- Specific weight is 8.92 g/cm^2.
- It possess high melting point near about 1300°C
- Maximum operating temperature is nearly 500°C.
- Its resistivity remains constant for wide range of temperatures.
- Resistivity is 0.48 – 0.52 Ω-mm^2/m.
- Temperature resistances coefficient 5.25×10^{-6} °C
- Tensile strength is 40 – 50 kg/mm^2.

Applications

- It is used for making rheostat coil and similar control devices.
- Constantan used to form thermocouples with wires made of iron, copper.

1.1.4 Nichrome

Nichrome is an alloy of nickel (75% – 80%), chromium (20 – 25%), manganin (1.5%) and a small amount of Ferrous. It is silver in appearance. It tends to be expensive due to high nickel content.

Properties

- High resistivity near about $1 - 1.11 \times 10^{-6}$ Ωm.
- Very high melting point (1350°C).
- Tensile strength is nearly equal to 75 kg/mm^2.
- Temperature coefficient of resistance is low.
- It with stand high temperature for longme without oxidising.
- High corrosion resistant property.
- Tensile strength is 65 – 70 kg/mm^2.

Applications

- It can be used as internal support structure in ceramics.
- Nichrome is widely used in explosives as a bridge wire in electric ignition system.
- It is used as heating element in electric heaters, furnaces and electric iron etc.

1.1.5 Tungsten

It is a steel grey colour metal which is brittle in nature.

Properties

- High melting point (3450°C).
- Boiling point is nearly 5950°C.
- Temperature coefficient of resistance is 0.00511.
- It is having high tensile strength.
- It is ductile in nature (can be drawn into very thick wires).
- Tungsten has lower coefficient of thermal expansion.
- Tungsten is chemically inert to acids and alkalis but oxidised in the presence of oxygen.
- Specific weight is 20 g/cm^3.
- Resistivity is 0.055 Ω-mm^2/m.
- Density is 19.3 g/cm^2.

Applications

- Tungsten is used in many high temperature applications such as light bulb, cathode ray tube and vacuum tube as filaments, heating elements and nozzles of rocket engines.
- Vibrators.
- It is used in battery ignition system, X-ray tubes, Magneto ignition systems.
- It is used for making glass to metal seals.

1.2 MATERIAL USED FOR FILAMENTS

A material used for making filaments must have the following properties

- High melting point.
- High mechanical strength.
- No tendency for oxidation.
- Ductility.
- Low resistance temperature coefficients.

Mostly Carbon, Tantalum and Tungsten are used as a filament material due to their following properties.

(a) Carbon

- High commercial efficiency about 3.8 to 4.6.
- Prevent blackening of the bulb.

(b) Tantalum

- Commercial efficiency about 3.5.
- High melting point near about 2800°C.
- Low resistivity and low temperature coefficient of resistance.

(c) Tangsten

- Melting point near about 3450°C
- Lumen efficiency is large.

Fig. 1.1 showing different shapes of filaments used in bulbs.

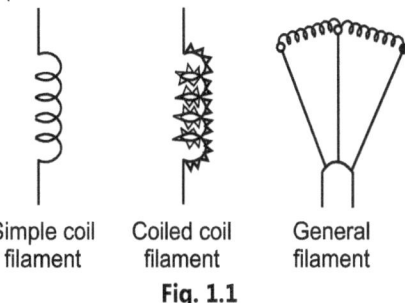

Simple coil   Coiled coil   General
filament   filament   filament

Fig. 1.1

1.2.1 Materials Used for Making Solders and Contacts

Solder is an alloy used to join two or more metals pieces. Melting point of solders is lower than materials to be joint. This process of joining pieces of metals is known as soldering. There are two types of solders.

(a) **Hard Solders :** It is normally alloy of Cu and Zn. It melt at very high temperature nearly higher than 400°C. It is mainly use for joining brass copper iron and steel.

(b) **Soft Solders :** Soft solder is an alloy of tin and lead. The most popular composition is 50% tin and 50% lead. This is use for working temperature lower than 400°C. It is used to join copper, bronze, brass, lead, tinned, iron, zinc etc.

1.2.2 Rewireable Fuse

Rewireable Fuse has Three Parts

1. **Base :** It consist of porcelain materials with fixed contacts which connected to live or phase wires.

2. **Fuse Carrier :** It is part which can be separate or taken out or insert in base with out any risk when switch is off.

3. **Fuse Wire**

   - Fuse wire is used depending on current ratting of the system.

   - Standard rating are 6, 16, 32, 63 and 100 A. It may use materials like lead, tinned, copper, aluminium or alloy of tin lead.

Advantages

   - Easy to operate.

   - Replacement is easy.

   - Reusable.

Mechanical Properties

   - High resistance against corrosion.

   - It should possess high mechanical strength.

   - It should be able to draw into thin wires i.e. it should be ductile.

   - It should be drawn into thin sheets i.e. it should be malleable.

   - Easy to fabricate.

   - Soldering welding of joints should have minimum contact resistance.

   - Durability and low cost.

1.2.3　Kanthal

It is an alloy of iron, chromium and aluminium.

Properties

- Low temperature coefficient of resistance.
- It withstands high temperature without oxidising.
- It has high melting point (1200°C).

Application

It is used in electric furnaces as a heating element.

1.2.4　Manganin

It is an alloy of Cu, manganese and nickel. It has the following properties.

Properties

- Its resistance is stable for long time.
- It has low temperature coefficient of resistance i.e. (0.00015/°C).
- It has high melting point (1020°C).
- Its resistivity is high 4.8×10^{-6} Ω-cm at 20°C.
- It is alloy of Cu – 80%, Mn – 17 to 18% and Ni – 1.5 to 2%.

Applications

It is used in standard resistance coil for instrument shunts, precision instruments, resistance boxes and bridge potentiometers etc.

1.2.5　Silver

Silver is having symbol Ag. It is having highest electrical conductivity of all elements.

Properties

- It absorbs free electrons.
- It is having low contact resistance.
- It is having highest electrical conductivity even greater than copper.
- High thermal conductivity.
- Ductile and malleable in nature.

Its resistivity is 1.59×10^{-6} Ω-cm at 20°C.

Applications

- Silver oxide batteries are used due to longer life and high energy / weight ratio.
- It is used in electrical contacts and conductors.
- It is used to make ornaments, jewellery, utensils and coins.
- As silver absorbs free electrons it is sometimes used as a control rods to regulate fission reaction.

1.3　COPPER ALLOYS

1.3.1　Brass

Brass is an alloy of copper and zinc. It is having bright gold like appearance.

Properties

- It is having 900 to 950°C melting point.
- It has high soldering and welding property.
- It has very good resistance to corrosion.
- Brass has low conductivity.
- It has greater mechanical strength and bearing resistance than copper.
- Brass has higher malleability than copper or zinc.

It's electrical resistivity is 9.1×10^{-6} Ω-cm at 20°C.

Applications

- Used for resistance welding.
- Brass can be used for making fan blades, fan cages and motor bearing.
- It is widely used in manufacture of electrical apparatus and current caring instruments.
- Brass can also be used for fixing for use in cryogenic systems.

1.3.2　Bronze

It is an alloy of copper and tin. It typically have 88% copper and 12% tin. It is hard and brittle material.

Properties

- Bronze is less brittle than iron.
- Bronzes are softer but heavier and have high mechanical strength.
- Metal to metal friction is less.
- Bronze containing copper, 0.9% cadmium have 85 to 95% conductivity to copper.
- Bronze containing copper, 0.8% cadmium, 0.6% tin has 50 to 80% conductivity as compared to copper.
- It is having high resistance to salt water corrosion.
- They are better conductor of heat and electricity.

Applications

- Bronze used as a heating element.
- It is used for making sliding contacts, current caring holders knife switch blades.
- It is used for making contact wires, commutator segments.

1.4   ELECTRIC FIELD AND SEMICONDUCTORS

Semiconductors are a group of materials having electrical conductivities intermediate between conductors and insulators. All the properties of conductors under static electric field hold for semiconductors, only they have less carriers inside them.

A perfect semiconductor crystal with no impurities or lattice defects is called an intrinsic semiconductor. In such materials there are no charge carriers at 0 K, so we will raise the temperature in order to create electron-hole pairs of such materials. In addition to that it is possible to create carriers in semiconductors by purposely introducing impurities into the crystal which is called doping. There are two types of doped semiconductors, n-type mostly electrons doped and p-type mostly holes doped. If we combine an n-type material and p-type material we will build a p-n junction.

P-N Junction and the Electric Field Inside

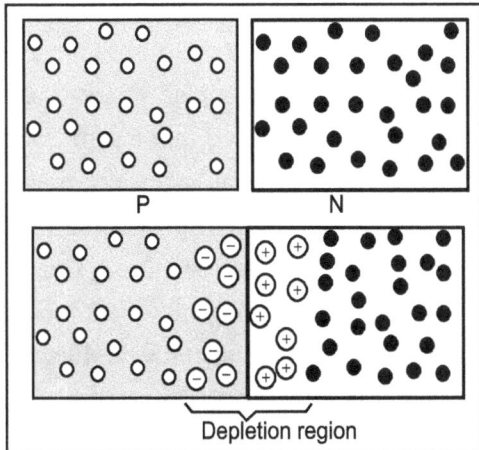

Fig. 1.2

In the above Fig. 1.2 shows when we combine the two materials electrons start diffusing from the n-type leaving positively charged ions to p-type and the opposite from p-type to n-type. But this situation does not last long as the increasing potential difference in the depletion region causes an electric field from the n-type material to the p-type material as shown in below Fig. 1.3.

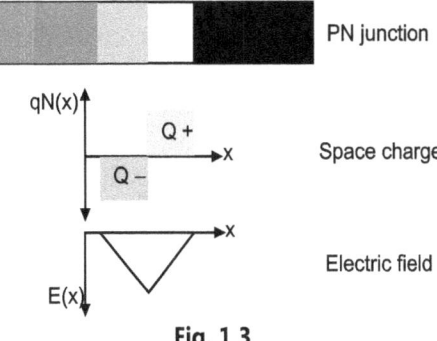

Fig. 1.3

The current due to diffusion of the charges is called the diffusion current which is from the p-type material to the n-type material. The current due to the electric field because the electric field pushes the positive charges to the p-type material and the negative charges to the n-type material is called the drift current. After a certain time these currents equal to each other in magnitude but in the opposite directions, however in the depletion region there is always carriers passing from one side to another.

There is current in the depletion region because of the carriers moving from one material to another, but there is no current outside this are so there is no electric field.

1.5   SUPERCONDUCTORS AND MAGNETIC FIELDS

In 1908 Heike Kammerlingh Onne succeeded in liquefying helium, which provided and ideal cold bath for experiments at temperatures close to absolute zero. In 1911 he made the discovery that when certain substances were cooled they act as superconductors. In 1933 Walter Meissner and Robert Ochsenfeld revealed that a superconducting material will repel a magnetic field. The reason behind this is that in a superconductor the induced currents exactly mirror the field that would have otherwise penetrated the superconducting material causing the magnet to be repulsed. This phenomenon is known as diamagnetism and is often referred as the "Meissner effect". The Meissner effect is so strong that a magnet can actually be levitated over a superconductive material. In 1962 scientists at Westinghouse developed the first commercial superconducting wire, an alloy of Niobium and Titanium. The first use of this wire in high-energy, particle-accelerator electromagnets, on the other hand, did not use until 1987 when it was used at the Fermilab Tevatron.

Superconductors are substances that conduct electricity without any resistance, when they are sufficiently cooled. Also, since there is no resistance in a super conductor, there is no heat dissipated by the super conductor. While there is no heat dissipated, there must not be any energy loss. This can be seen from the fact that V/I is proportional to the volume integral of J.E. (energy), where J and E are the conduction current density and the electromotive intensity. The conductance in a super conductor goes to infinity, because of the fact that

G = 1/R where G is the conductance and R is the resistance.

A superconductor will not allow any magnetic field to freely enter in it. This is because microscopic magnetic dipoles are induced in the superconductor that opposes the applied field.

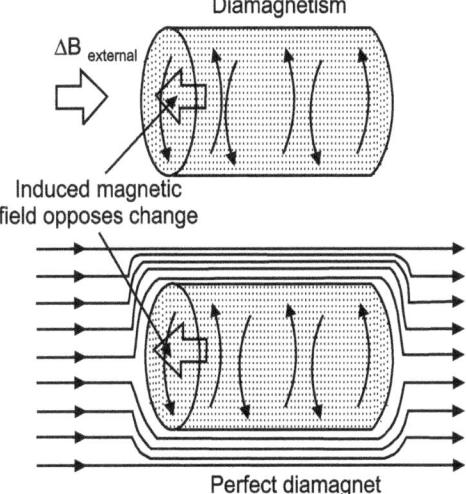

Fig. 1.4

This induced field then repels the source of the applied field, and will consequently drive back the magnet associated with that field. This implies that if a magnet was placed on top of the superconductor when the superconductor was above its Critical Temperature (Tc), and then it was cooled down to below Tc, the superconductor would then exclude the magnetic field of the magnet. This can be seen quite clearly since a magnet itself is repelled, and thus is levitated above the superconductor.

1.5.1 Type I Superconductors

There are two types of Superconductors Type I & Type II. The Type I category of superconductors is mainly comprised of metals and metalloids that show some conductivity at room temperature. Type 1 superconductors are characterized as the "soft" super conductors and show a very sharp transition to a superconducting state.

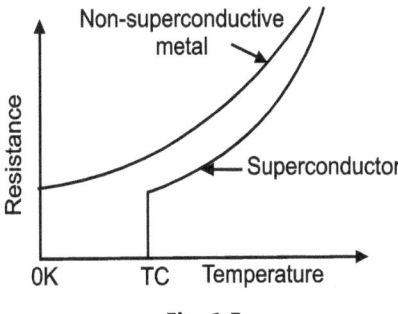

Fig. 1.5

They require the coldest temperatures to become superconductive and to slow down molecular vibrations sufficiently to facilitate unimpeded electron flow in accordance with it as per BCS theory. BCS theory suggests that electrons team up in Cooper pairs in order to help each other overcome molecular obstacles.

This process is called as phonon-mediated coupling. Type I super conductors have one critical magnetic field for any given temperature. If they are in a magnetic field that is weaker than the critical magnetic field, they have zero resistance and show ideal diamagnetism. If the magnetic field is stronger than the critical magnetic field, resistance is greater than zero, and there is flux penetration. below table give list of Type I super conductors and their critical temperature.

following graph is showing a Type I superconductor and the measured $\mu_0 M$ where M = Magnetization versus an applied magnetic field.

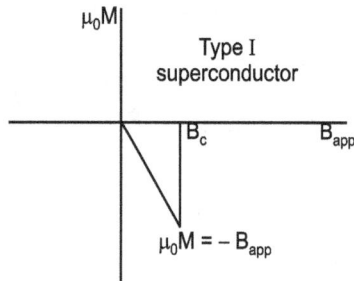

Fig. 1.6

Table 1.1

Material	Tc
Carbon ©	15 K
Lead (Pb)	7.196 K
Tantalum (Ta)	4.47 K
Mercury (Hg)	4.15 K
Tin (Sn)	3.72 K
Indium (In)	3.41 K
Thallium (Tl)	2.38 K
Rhenium (Re)	1.697 K
Protactinium (Pa)	1.40 K
Gallium (Ga)	1.083 K
Molybdenum (Mo)	0.915 K
Thorium (Th)	1.38 K
Aluminum (Al)	1.175 K
Zinc (Zn)	0.85 K

Osmium (Os)	0.66 K
Zirconium (Zr)	0.61 K
Americium (Am)	0.60 K
Cadmium (Cd)	0.517 K
Ruthenium (Ru)	0.49 K
Titanium (Ti)	0.40 K
Uranium (U)	0.20 K
Hafnium (Hf)	0.128 K
Iridium (Ir)	0.1125 K
Lutetium (Lu)	0.100 K
Beryllium (Be)	0.026 K
Tungsten (W)	0.0154 K
Platinum (Pt)	0.0019 K

1.5.2 Type II Superconductors

Except for the elements vanadium, technetium and niobium, the Type 2 category of superconductors is comprised of metallic compounds and alloys. The recently discovered superconducting "perovskites" metal-oxide ceramics that normally have a ratio of 2 metal atoms to every 3 oxygen atoms fit in to this Type 2 group. They achieve higher Tc's than Type 1 superconductors by a mechanism that is still not completely understood. Conventional wisdom holds that it relates to the planar layering within the crystalline structure. The superconducting cuprates (copper oxides) have achieved astonishingly high Tc's when consider at 1985 known Tc's had only reached 23 K. now, the highest Tc attained at ambient pressure has been 138K. One theory predicts an upper limit of about 200 K for the layered cuprates. Others assert there is no limit. moreover, it is almost certain that other more synergistic compounds still look forward to discovery among the high-temperature superconductors. Type 2 superconductors also known as the "hard" superconductors differ from Type 1 in that their transition from a normal to a superconducting state is gradual across a region of "mixed state". A Type 2 will also permit some penetration by an external magnetic field into its surface. Type II superconductors have two critical magnetic fields, Bc1<Bc2. For a magnetic field B less than Bc1, the superconductor acts like a type I, and for a magnetic field B greater than Bc2, the substance behaves as a normal material. A unique phenomenon occurs when the magnetic field is between Bc1 and Bc2. In this case, the superconductor has zero resistance but allows partial flux penetration. This is supposed to

be the vortex state. In the vortex state there are cores of normal material, surrounded by material in the superconducting state. As the magnetic field increases, the number of normal cores increases until eventually, the material becomes non-superconducting. below table give list of some Type II super conductors.

Compound	Tc
$HgBa_2Ca_2Cu_3O_8$	133K
$HgBa_2Ca_3Cu_4O_{10}$	127K
$SmBaSrCu_{3O7}$	86K
$HgBa_2CuO_4$	94K
$Tl_2Ba_2Ca_3Cu_4O_{10}$	128K
$Tl_2Ba_2CaCu_3O^8$	119K
$TlBa_2Ca_2Cu_3O_8$	110K
$TlBa_2CaCu_2O_7$	92K
$Bi_2CaSr_2Cu_2O_8$	92K
$Bi_2Ca_2Sr_2Cu_3O_{10}$	110K
$YBa_2Cu_3O_7$	93K

fig. is showing a Type II superconductor and the measured μ_0M (M = Magnetization) versus an applied magnetic field

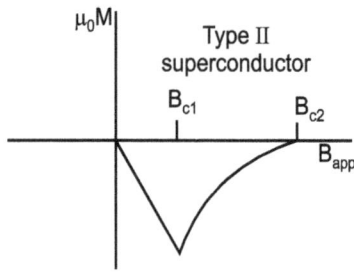

Fig. 1.7

1.5.3 Applications of Superconductors

Electric Power

High Temperature superconductors can be used in the production of more cost effective motors and generators. Also High temperature superconductor power cables can carry 2 to 10 times more power in equally or smaller sized cables, since the fact that with zero resistance there is no heat loss during the transmission of current over the transmission lines. A superconductivity technology depends on whether wires can be prepared from the brittle ceramics that retain their superconductivity at 77 K while supporting large current densities.

Cutaway of HTS Power Transmission Cable

Following fig. Shows how Liquid nitrogen circulates through the hollow core of an High temperature Superconductor assembly, which is enclosed by layers of thermal and electrical insulation encapsulated in an outer steel jacket. Cable cross-section

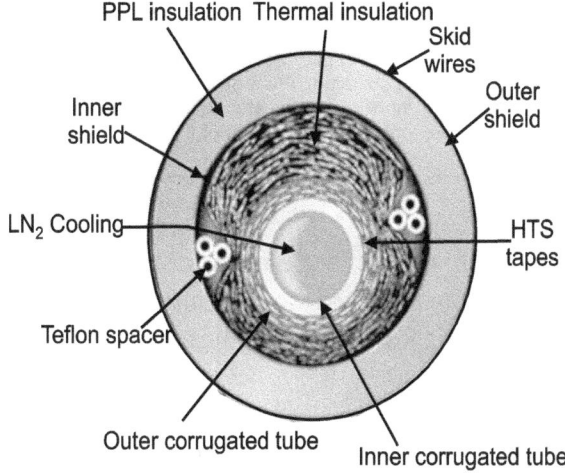

Fig. 1.8

Transportation

The use of superconductors for transportation has already been established using liquid helium as a refrigerant. Prototype levitated trains have been constructed in Japan by using superconducting magnets. High temperature superconductor coils create strong magnetic fields that produce the effect of levitation by repulsion or attraction. This is the principle underlying magnetically levitated or maglev trains. Maglev trains hover above a magnetic field without any physical contact with a track during operation. As a result, high speeds of up to 500 miles per hour are possible with only a small consumption of energy.

Medical Industry

Magnetic resonance imaging (MRI) is playing an ever growing role in diagnostic medicine. Superconductive magnetic coils are an important portion of this whole body scanner. Since these coils are capable of producing very stable, large magnetic field strengths, they generate high quality images. Currently, low temperature superconductors are employed in these coils, but the ultimate use of High Temperature Superconductor materials will significantly enhance the cost-benefit aspect of the application.

1.6   BIMETALLIC STRIPS

Bonding two metals with different thermal expansion coefficients can produce useful devices for detecting and measuring temperature changes. A typical pair is brass and steel with typical expansion coefficients of 19 and 13 parts per million per degree Celsius respectively.

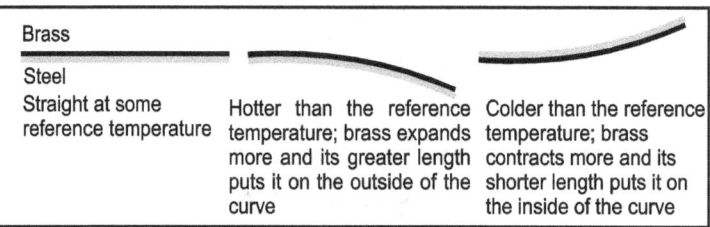

Fig. 1.9

The examples shown are straight strips, but bimetallic strips are made in coils to increase their sensitivity used in thermostats. One of the many uses for bimetallic strips is in electrical breakers where excessive current through the strip heats it and bends it to trip the switch to interrupt the current.

1.7   THERMOCOUPLE

A thermocouple is a device used widely for measuring temperature. A thermocouple is comprised of at least two metals joined together to form two junctions. One is connected to the body whose temperature is to be measured; this is called hot or measuring junction. The other junction is connected to a body of known temperature; this is called cold or reference junction. as a result the thermocouple measures unknown temperature of the body with reference to the known temperature of the other body.

Working Principle

The working principle of thermocouple is based on three effects, revealed by Seebeck, Peltier and Thomson. They are as follows

- **Seebeck Effect :** The Seebeck effect states that when two different or unlike metals are joined together at two junctions, an electromotive force is generated at the two junctions. The amount of emf generated is different for different combinations of the metals.

- **Peltier Effect :** As per the Peltier effect, when two different or unlike metals are joined together to form two junctions, emf is generated within the circuit due to the different temperatures of the two junctions of the circuit.

- **Thomson Effect :** As per the Thomson effect, when two different or unlike metals are joined together forming two junctions, the potential exists within the circuit due to temperature gradient along the entire length of the conductors within the circuit.

In most of the cases the emf suggested by the Thomson effect is very small and it can be neglected by making proper selection of the metals. The Peltier effect plays a important role in the working principle of the thermocouple.

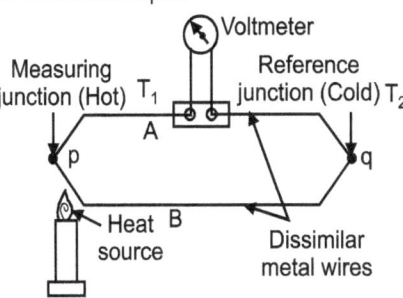

Fig. 1.10

Working

The general circuit for the working of thermocouple is shown in the fig. 1 above. It consist of two dissimilar metals, A and B. These are joined together to form two junctions, p and q, which are maintained at the temperatures T1and T2 respectively. keep in mind that the thermocouple cannot be formed if there are not two junctions. Since the two junctions are maintained at different temperatures. the Peltier emf is generated within the circuit . it is the function of the temperatures of two junctions.

If the temperature of both the junctions is same, equal and opposite emf will be generated at both junctions and the net current flowing through the junction is zero. If the junctions are maintained at different temperatures, the emf's will not become zero and there will be a net current flowing through the circuit. The total emf flowing through this circuit depends on the metals used within the circuit as well as the temperature of the two junctions. The total emf or the current flowing through the circuit can be measured easily.

The device for measuring the current or emf is connected within the circuit of the thermocouple. It measures the amount of emf flowing through the circuit due to the two junctions of the two dissimilar metals maintained at different temperatures. Now, the temperature of the reference junctions is already known, while the temperature of measuring junction is unknown. The output obtained from the thermocouple circuit is calibrated against the unknown temperature. Thus the voltage or current output obtained from thermocouple circuit gives the value of unknown temperature directly.

Types of thermocouple

J type :	0°C to 750°C
K type :	−200°C to 1250°C
E type :	−200°C to 900°C
T type :	250°C to 350°C

1.8 FREE ELECTRON THEORY OF METALS

Classical Free Electron Theory of Metals

Classical free electron theory is also known as Drude-Lorentz theory as it was developed by Drude and Lorentz. Drude proposed an exceedingly simple model that explained a well-known empirical law, the Wiedermann{Franz law (1853). This law stated that at a given temperature the ratio of the thermal conductivity to the electrical conductivity was the same for all metals. P.Drude suggested that the transport properties of metals might be understood by assuming that their electrons are free and in thermal equilibrium with their atoms. This theory was made more quantitative by H.A. Lorentz. Following are the assumptions made in this theory

- A metal is imagined as a structure of 3-dimensional array of ions between which there are freely moving valence electrons confined to the body of the material.

- Mutual repulsion between electrons is ignored and hence potential energy is taken as zero. Therefore the total energy of the electron is equal to its kinetic energy.

- The free electrons are treated as equivalent to gas molecules and thus they are assumed to obey the laws of kinetic theory of gases. In the absence of field, the energy associated with each electron at a temperature T is given by 3/2 kT.

Free Electron Concept : All metal atoms consist of valence electrons. They are responsible for electrical conduction. Valence electrons are loosely bound to the nucleus. When a large number of atoms join to form a metal, the boundaries of the neighboring atoms overlap. Valence electrons can move easily throughout the body of the metal. These electrons are called free electrons or conduction electrons which account for properties such as electrical conductivity, thermal conductivity, opacity, surface luster etc.

Drift Velocity : If electric field is not applied to a conductor, the free electrons move in random directions. They collide with each other. They also with the positive ions. Since the motion is completely random, average velocity in any direction is zero. If a constant electric field is established inside a conductor, the electrons experience a force

$$F = -eE$$

This is due to which they move in the direction opposite to direction of the field. These electrons undergo frequent collisions with positive ions. In each collision, direction of motion of electrons undergoes random changes. In addition to the random motion, the electrons are subjected to a very slow directional motion. This motion is called drift and the average velocity of this motion is called drift velocity vd.

Consider a conductor subjected to an electric field E in the x-direction. The force on the electron due to the electric field = -eE.

As per Newton's law,

$$-eE = m \, d \, vd/dt$$
$$d \, vd = -eEdt/m$$

Integrating,

$$Vd = -eEt/m + Constant$$

When t = 0, vd = 0

Thus, Constant = 0

$$Vd = -eEt/m \tag{1.1}$$

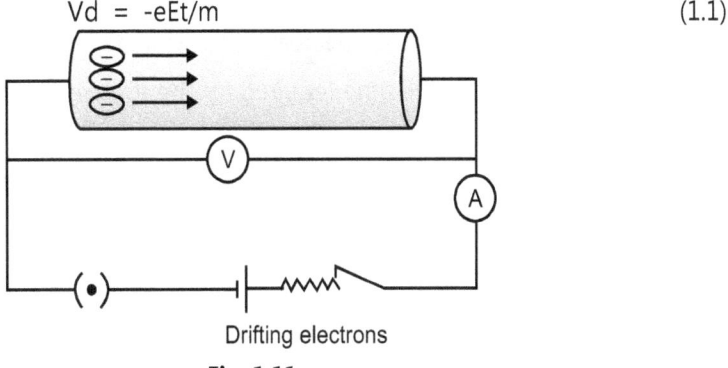

Drifting electrons

Fig. 1.11

Electrical Conductivity

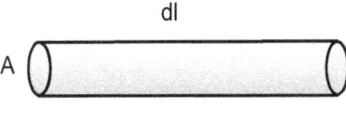

Fig. 1.12

Consider a wire of length 'dl' and

area of cross section = 'A' subjected to an electric field E.

concentration of the electrons = 'n'

the number of electrons flowing through the wire in dt seconds = nAvddt.

The quantity of charge flowing in time dt = nAvddt.e

Therefore I = dq/dt = neAvd

Current density J = I/A = nevd

Subsittuting the value of vd from (1.1),

$$J = nee \, Et/m = ne2Et/m \tag{1.2}$$

By Ohm's law, $J = sE$

Therefore $s = J/E = ne2t/m$ (1.3)

Mobility of a charge carrier is the ratio of the drift mobility to the electric field.

$$\mu = vd/E \ m2/Volt\text{-}Sec$$

Put vd from (1.1),

$$\mu = et/m$$ (1.4)

Put this in equation (1.3),

$$s = ne\mu$$ (1.5)

Relaxation Time and Mean Free Path

Now the field E is turned off. Due to the collision of the electrons with lattice ions and lattice defects, their velocity will start to decrease. This process is called relaxation.

Relaxation Time(t) : It is the time required for the drift velocity to reduce to 1/e of its initial value.

Mean Free Path (l) of the Electron : It is the average distance traveled by an electron between two consecutive collisions

$$l = vdt$$ (1.6)

Temperature Dependence

The free electron theory is based on Maxwell-Boltzmann statistics.

Kinetic energy of electron = $\frac{1}{2} m(Vd)^2 = 3/2 \ KBT$

$$Vd = Ö \ 3KBT/m$$

Substituting this in equation (1.6),

$$t = l \ Ö \ m/3KBT$$ (1.7)

$$s = ne2t/m,$$

s is proportional to $Ö(1/T)$

r is proportional to $ÖT$.

Disadvantages of Classical Free Electron Theory

- Classical theory failed to explain the variation of electronic specific heat at low temperatures.

- The mean free path of electrons in any metal, calculated on the basis of Drude's model was ten times less than the experimentally observed value.

- The Lorenz number, L calculated for many metals using the standard relation is equal to $2.45 \times 10{-8}$ watt m/K^2. However, for many metals, the Lorentz number varies with temperature at low temperatures. This is due to the fact all the electrons may not be participating in conduction process.

- Drude's classical free electron theory totally failed to explain the conduction mechanism in semiconductors and insulators.

- The classical model could not explain the origin of Pauli's paramagnetism.

- This theory fails to explain ferromagnetism, superconductivity, photoelectric effect, Compton effect and blackbody radiation.

We shall now discuss one or two failures of classical free electron theory of metals with necessary theory.

1.8.1 Quantum Free Electron Theory

In 1928, Sommerfeld developed a new theory, in which he retained some of the features of classical free electron theory and included quantum mechanical concepts and Fermi-Dirac statistics to the free electrons in the metal. This theory is called quantum free electron theory. Quantum free electron theory permits only a fraction of electrons to gain energy.

Assumptions of this theory are

- The energy values of conduction electrons are quantized and are realized in terms of a set of energy levels.

- The distribution of electrons in various allowed energy levels takes place according to Pauli's exclusion principle

- The electrons move in a constant potential inside the metal and are confined within defined boundaries.

- The attraction between the electrons and the lattice ions and the repulsion between the electrons themselves are ignored.

Quantum free electron theory permits only a fraction of electrons to gain energy.

In order to determine the actual number of electrons in a given energy range(dE), it is necessary to know the number of states(dNs) which have energy in that range.

Density of States : The number of states per unit energy range is called the density of states g(E).

$$g(E) = dNs/dE$$

According to Fermi-Dirac statistics, the probability that a particular energy state with energy E is occupied by an electron is given by,

$$f(E) = 1 / [1+e(E-EF/KT)]$$

where EF is called Fermi level.

Energy corresponding to Fermi level is known as Fermi energy. Fermi level is the highest filled energy level at 0 K. Now the actual number of electrons present in the energy range dE,

$$dN = f(E) \, g(E) dE$$

Effect of Temperature on Fermi-Dirac Distribution Function

Fermi-Dirac distribution function is given by,

$$f(E) = 1 / [1 + e(E - EF/KT)]$$

At T=0K, for EEF, f(E)=0

At T=0K, for E=EF, f(E)=indeterminate

At T>0K, for E=EF, f(E)=1/2

Fig.1.13 below shows the effect of temperature on fermi level.

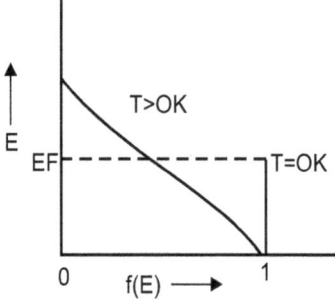

Fig. 1.13

Disadvantages of Quantum Free Electron Theory

- It fails to explain properties of metal alloys.
- It fails to explain why only some solids are metals and others are either semiconductors or insulators.

1.8.2 Difference between Classical Free Electron Theory and Quantum Free Electron Theory

Sr. no.	Classical Free Electron Theory	Quantum Free Electron Theory
1.	free electrons obey Maxwell-Boltzman statistics	free electrons obey Fermi-Dirac statistics.
2.	free electrons can possess any energy values	free electrons can occupy certain energy levels with discrete energy values
3.	it is possible that many electrons possessing same energy.	Free electrons obey Pauli's exclusion

1.9 THERMAL CONDUCTIVITY

The thermal conductivity is the ratio of the thermal current to the magnitude of the temperature gradient. In the presence of a temperature gradient $\frac{\partial T}{\partial x}$, the average thermal energy $<\frac{1}{2}m\upsilon_T^2>$ will depend on the local temperature T(x). The electrons sense the local temperature through collisions with the lattice. Thus, the thermal energy of a given electron will depend on where it made its last collision. Therefore, an electron crossing the plane $x = x_0$ at an angle μ to the x-axis had its last collision at $x = x_0 - {}^{\upsilon}T^{\tau} \cos \theta$.

The energy of such an electron is

$$E(x) = E(x_0 - {}^{\upsilon}T^{\tau} \cos \theta)$$

The number of electrons per unit volume whose direction of motion is in the solid angle d- is $\eta_0 \frac{d\Omega}{4\pi}$

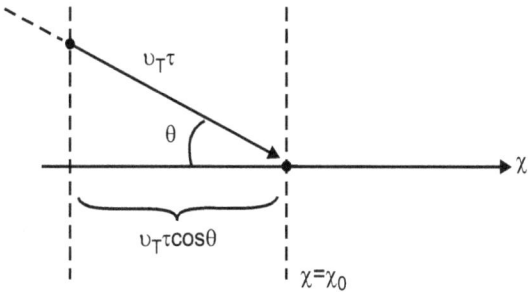

Fig. 1.14

electron crossing the plane x = x0 at angle θ to the x-axis

The number of such electrons crossing a unit area at x0 is $\eta_0 \frac{d\Omega}{4\pi} {}^{\upsilon}T \cos \theta$,

giving

$$w(x_0) = \int E(x0 - {}^{\upsilon}T^{\tau} \cos \theta) \eta_0 {}^{\upsilon}T \cos \theta \frac{d\Omega}{4\pi}.$$

for the energy °ux through a unit area at x0

$$w(x) = -\frac{1}{3} \eta_0 \upsilon_T^2 \tau \left(\frac{\partial E}{\partial x}\right).$$

the integral over μ from 0 to ¼ gives

$$E (x_0 - {}^{\upsilon}T^{\tau} \cos \theta)$$

$$\frac{\partial E}{\partial x} = \frac{\partial E}{\partial T} \frac{\partial T}{\partial x'}$$

But

$$K = \frac{\omega}{-\partial T/\partial x} = \frac{1}{3}\eta_0 v_T^2 \tau \frac{dE}{dT} = \frac{1}{3}v_T^2 \tau C_v,$$

so the thermal conductivity is given by

where
$$C_v = \eta_0 \frac{dE}{dT}$$

is the heat capacity per unit volume

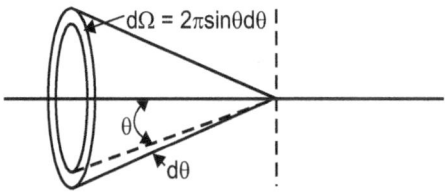

Fig. 1.15

Solid angle $d\Omega$ in which electrons moving to cross the plane x = x_0 at an angle θ to the x-axis

1.9.1 Temperature Dependence of Conductivity

In most solids the two main types of internal energy are

- the vibrational energy of the atoms about their mean lattice positions
- the kinetic energy of the free electrons.
- If heat is supplied to the body its temperature rises and the internal energy increases.
- The important thermal properties of matter such as heat capacity, thermal expansion and thermal conductivity depend upon the changes in the energy of the atoms and free electrons. If an electrical field is applied to a solid the free electrons are accelerated.
- Their kinetic energy increases. Some of this kinetic energy is of course lost by collisions with the atoms in the lattice.
- The resulting current is proportional to the average velocity of the free electrons. This velocity is determined by the applied electrical field and also the collision frequency.
- The drift velocity (vd) which is superimposed on a much higher velocity called root mean square velocity due to the random motion of the electron which is possible even in the absence of the electric field.
- The random motion, which contributes zero current, exists also in the presence of the field. In the absence of an electric field the free electrons in a metal will be moving about at random in all directions and will be in temperature equilibrium with it. If the mass of an electron is m then at absolute temperature T it will possess an average random velocity given by the kinetic theory of gases. Thus $\frac{1}{2}m\bar{c}^2 = \frac{3}{2}kT$

where k is the Boltzmann constant. Now an electric field E is applied. Under the influence of this field the electron acquires a drift velocity. The resulting acceleration of the electron is $\dfrac{eE}{m}$ where eE is the force acting on the electron and m is the mass of the electron. The drift velocity is much smaller compared to random velocity. Further the drift velocity is not retained after a collision with an atom because of the relatively large mass. Hence just after a collision the drift velocity is zero.

1.9.2 Thermoelectric Effect

It is a phenomenon related to the thermal conductivity of electrons in that it too is a consequence of the drift of electrons under a thermal gradient. These are two aspects to thermoelectric phenomena.

- **Seeback Effect :** A temperature between the two junctions of two dissimilar materials gives rise to an emf in the circuit.
- **Peltier Effect :** if a current is circulated in a circuit consisting of two dissimilar materials, is liberated at one junction and absorbed at the other.

Both effects are the subject of considerable study because of their practical applications. The generation of electrical power using the Seeback effect offers the desirable freedom from removing parts, and similar advantages are available in the use of the Peltier effect in refrigeration. In either case one of the main considerations is the size of the effect, which is a consequence of the detailed electronic structure of the two materials, and a simple theoretical treatment is not available. The parameters of the material which are significant in this respect are the same as for the conductivity, namely the effective mass of the electrons and the relaxation time. Thermoelectric effects of either sign can be observed, depending mainly on whether electron effects or hole effects are predominant. By careful selection of the parameters using doped semiconductors, thermoelectric power supplies now have efficiencies approacting 20% and thermoelectric refrigerators have been built which can maintains a temperature 50°F below room temperature.

The most familiar example of a metal-metal junction is the thermocouple, which is made of a configuration of the type A-B-A. If a current is passed through such a combination, the temperature of one of the functions is found to rise and that of the other to fall. This is called the Peltier effect. Conversely, if one junction is heated and the other cooled, a p.d develops across the combination. This is called Seeback effect.

1.9.3 Wiedemann-Franz Law

Relation Between Thermal Conductivity and Electrical Conductivity

Fig. 1.16 shows the view of a copper rod of appreciable length with unit area of cross-section in the steady state.

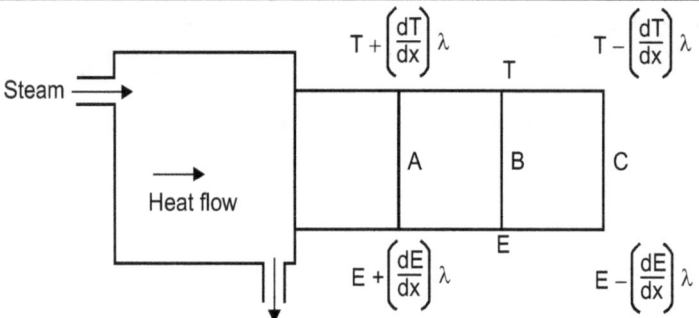

Fig. 1.16 : Flow of heat through a copper rod at the steady state

Let λ = AB = BC be the mean free path of the electron.

The excess of energy carried by an electron from A to B is $\left[\dfrac{dE}{dx}\right]\lambda$.

Hence the excess of energy transported by the process of conduction through unit area in unit time at the middle layer B is $\dfrac{n\bar{c}\lambda}{6}\left[\dfrac{dE}{dx}\right]$.

Deficit of energy transported through B in the opposite direction is $\dfrac{1}{6}\,n\bar{c}\lambda\left[\dfrac{dE}{dx}\right]$

Let us assume $\dfrac{1}{6}\,n\bar{c}$ is the number of free electrons flowing in a given direction through unit area in unit time.

Thus the net energy transported through unit area in unit time from A to B is

$$\frac{1}{6}\,n\bar{c}\lambda\left[\frac{dE}{dx}\right]-\left[\frac{1}{6}\,n\bar{c}\lambda\left[\frac{dE}{dx}\right]=\frac{n\bar{c}\lambda}{3}\left(\frac{dE}{dT}\right)\left(\frac{dT}{dx}\right)\right]$$

The general expression for the quantity of heat energy transported through unit area for unit time is $\sigma_T\left(\dfrac{dT}{dX}\right)$.

Equating the two equations, one gets $\sigma_T = \dfrac{n\bar{c}\lambda}{3}\left(\dfrac{dE}{dT}\right)$

But $\dfrac{dE}{dT}$ is the energy required to raise the temperature by one degree and hence it is $[cv]_{el.}$

Now
$$\boxed{\sigma T = \frac{n\,\bar{c}\,\lambda}{3}\,[C_v]_{el} = \frac{n\lambda[C_v]_{el}}{3}\sqrt{\frac{3k\,T}{m}}}$$

But $\qquad\qquad [C_v]_{el} = \dfrac{3}{2}\,k$ with n = 1 electron

---

Thus

$$\sigma_T = \frac{n\lambda}{3}\left(\frac{3}{2}k\right)\sqrt{\frac{3kT}{m}} = \frac{n\lambda k}{2}\sqrt{\frac{3kT}{m}}$$

$$\sigma = \frac{ne^2\lambda}{\sqrt{12mkT}}$$

$$\frac{\sigma_T}{\sigma} = \frac{n\lambda k}{2}\sqrt{\frac{3kT}{m}}\left\{\frac{\sqrt{12mkT}}{ne^2\lambda}\right\}$$

$$\boxed{\frac{\sigma_T}{\sigma} = 3\left[\frac{k}{e}\right]^2 T}$$

This is called Wiedemann Franz law and the multiplying factor 3 (k/e)2 is called Lorentz number.

Wiedmann-Franz Law : The ratio of thermal conductivity to electrical conductivity of a metal is directly proportional to absolute temperature.

1.9.4 Joule's Law

Heat Developed in Current Carrying Conductor

The heat developed in a current carrying conductor is given by

$$H = I^2R = \frac{V^2}{R}$$

$$H = \frac{(El)^2}{\rho\frac{l}{A}} = \frac{E^2Al}{\rho}$$

$$H = \sigma E^2 Al$$

Thus heat developed per unit volume per second is

$$W = \sigma E^2$$

current density

$$j = \sigma E$$

$$W = \frac{jE^2}{E} = jE = \sigma E^2$$

In an isotropic medium, consider a particular electron which at the instant t = 0, has carried out a collision with the lattice, and let the velocity components of the electron be vx, vy and vz.

Now at the instant (t > 0), the electron has yet to collide with the lattice again, and an electric field of intensity E is applied along the negative x-direction, the velocity components of the electron are $v_x + \left(\dfrac{e}{m}\right) Et$. The increment $\left[\dfrac{e}{m} Et\right]$ in velocity is due to the acceleration due to the field on the electron.

Thus the increase in energy of the electron over the field is

$$(\Delta W)_t = \frac{1}{2} m \left[\left\{ v_x + \frac{e}{m} Et \right\}^2 - v_x^2 \right]$$

$$(\Delta W)_t = \frac{1}{2} m \left[\left[\frac{2e}{m} \right] E\, v_x t + \left[\frac{e}{m} \right]^2 E^2 t^2 \right]$$

The above expression may be averaged over a large number of electrons without having suffered a collision, but which have a random distribution of their velocities. Thus are finds

$$(\Delta W)_t = \frac{1}{2} m \left(\frac{e}{m} \right)^2 E^2 t^2 = \frac{e^2 E t^2}{2m}$$

If P (t) represents the probability that an electron moves for a ture t without suffering a collision, then P(t) = exp (–t/τ_c). For isotropic scattering, the average time between collisions, is equal to the relaxation time τ. Also, the probability that an electron will suffer a collision during a time dt is given by

$$\frac{dt}{\tau_c} = \frac{dt}{\tau}$$

So, the probability that the electron makes a collisions between t and t + dt is given by

$$\left[\exp\left(\frac{-t}{\tau}\right) \right] \left(\frac{dt}{\tau} \right)$$

Thus, the average energy increase of the electrons during the period between two collisions is equal to

$$(\Delta W) = \int_{t=0}^{\infty} (\Delta W)_t \exp\left(\frac{-t}{\tau}\right) \frac{dt}{\tau}$$

$$= \left[\frac{e^2 E^2}{2m\tau} \right] \int_0^{\infty} t^2 e^{\frac{-t}{\tau}}\, dt$$

We known that

$$\int_0^{\infty} x^n e^{-ax}\, dx = \frac{\angle n}{a^{n+1}}$$

$$\Delta W = \frac{e^2 E^2 \tau^2}{m}$$

If n is the number of electrons present in unit volume, the total energy dissipated per unit volume per second

$$W = \frac{n}{\tau} \Delta W$$

$$W = \frac{n}{\tau} \frac{e^2 E^2 \tau^2}{m} = \sigma E^2$$

This agrees with the experimental work.

1.10 FUSE

Fuse is a type of low resistance resistor which provides over current protection, of either the load or source circuit. Fuse is composed of an alloy which has a low melting point. A strip of this fuse is placed in series with the circuit. The working principle is that if the current is in excess then the strip would melt and break the circuit. There are different variants of fuse boxes available with different types of circuit breaking. Slow blow fuses are designed to allow higher currents for a modest amount of time longer, and such considerations are and were commonly necessary when electronics devices or systems had electronic tube tech or a large number of incandescent lights were being powered such as in a large hall, theater or stadium. Tubes and incandescent lights each have reduced current needs as they heat up to operating temperatures for their internal resistance grows as they are heated the same physics principle causes the fuse material to melt, disconnecting the circuit from power.

Other fuse boxes are designed to break the circuit rapidly. The selection is based upon the kind of device and also the fluctuation level of the current.

Construction

The fuse element is made of zinc, copper, silver, aluminum, or alloys to provide stable and predictable characteristics. A fuse consists of a metal strip or wire fuse element, of small cross-section compared to the circuit conductors, mounted between a pair of electrical terminals, and enclosed by a non-combustible housing. The fuse is arranged in series to carry all the current passing through the protected circuit. The resistance of the element generates heat due to the current flow. The size and construction of the element is determined so that the heat produced for a normal current does not cause the element to attain a high temperature Fuses can be built with different sized enclosures to prevent interchange of different ratings or types of fuse. For example, bottle style fuses distinguish between ratings with different cap diameters. Automotive glass fuses were made in different lengths, to prevent high-rated fuses being installed in a circuit intended for a lower rating

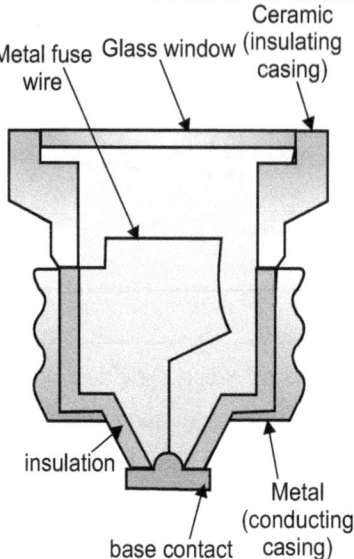

Fig. 1.17

The main components of a standard fuse unit consist of the following items

- Metal fuse element
- Set of contacts
- Support body

Types of Fuse

The major two categories of fuses include

- **Low Voltage Fuses :** In this category all fuses up to 1.5 kV can be included. But the most typical voltage levels for low voltage fuses are 500 V, 690 V and 750 V. LV HRC fuses are used for installation systems in non-residential, commercial and industrial buildings, as well as in the switchboards of power supply companies. They protect essential building parts and installations. In order to understand Low voltage fuses better, we can further classify it further into

- **Semi Enclosed or Rewireable Type :** This is also called as the KIT-KAT type fuse. This fuse is most commonly used in the case of domestic wiring and small scale usage. The main composition is of a porcelain base which holds the wires. The fuse element is located inside a carrier that is also made out of porcelain.

The main metals or alloys used in making fuse wire include lead, tinned copper, aluminum or tin lead alloy. The main advantage of this type of fuse is that it is easy to install and also replace without risking any electrical injury. But there is a level of lack of discrimination and a small time lag, which may deter its functionality. With a slow speed of operation, it has low rupturing capacity.

Fig. 1.18 : Rewireable fuse

- **Totally Enclosed or Cartridge Type :** In this type of fuse, there is a completely closed container and contacts are on either side. They are sub divided into following types

- **D Type :** This cannot be interchanged and comes with the following main components fuse base and cap, adapter ring and the cartridge. The fuse base has the cap screwed to it and the cartridge is pushed into it. The circuit becomes complete when the tip of the cartridge is in contact with the conductor.

- **Link Type :** When it comes to current distribution, there is need for a specified break capacity of high nature. This is where the alternate name of this fuse High Rapturing Capacity comes from. The fusing factor in such cases is up to 1.45.

Link type are further sub divided into knife blade type and bolted type.

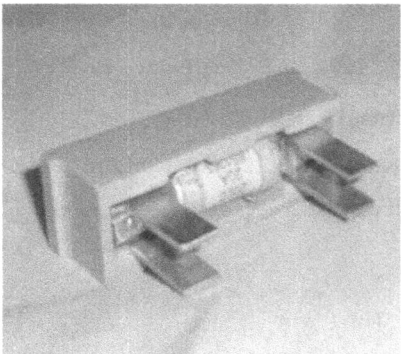

Fig. 1.19 : Totally enclosed or cartridge type

- **High Voltage Fuses :** All fuses used on power systems from 1.5 kV up to 138 kV are categorized as high voltage fuses. Large power fuses use fusible elements made of silver, copper or tin to provide stable and predictable performance. High voltage expulsion fuses surround the fusible link with gas-evolving substances, such as boric acid. When the fuse blows, heat from the arc causes the boric acid to evolve large volumes of gases. The associated high pressure (often greater than

100 atmospheres) and cooling gases rapidly quench the resulting arc. The hot gases are then explosively expelled out of the end(s) of the fuse. Such fuses can only be used outdoors.

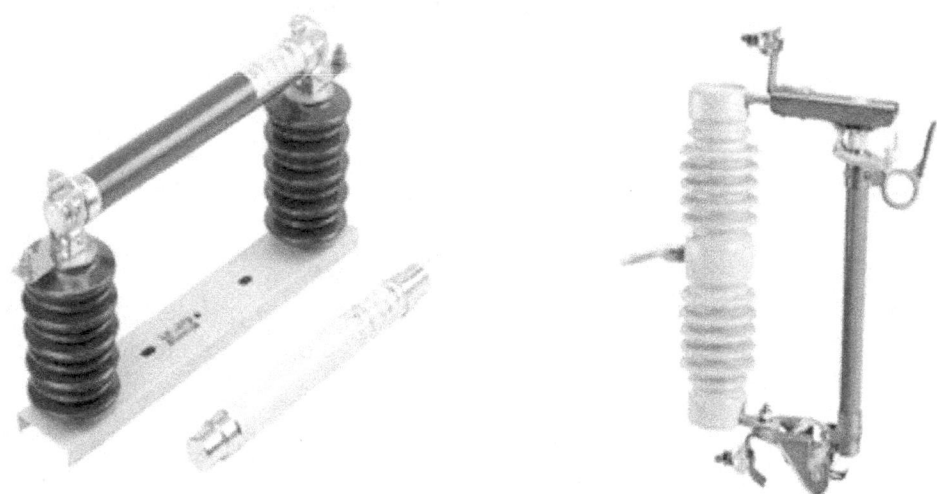

Fig. 1.20 : High voltage fuse

High voltage high power fuses are standalone protective switching devices used to 138 kV. They are used in power supply networks and for distribution uses. The most frequent application is in transformer circuits, with further uses in motor circuits and capacitor banks. These type of fuses may have an impact pin to operate a switch mechanism, so that all three phases are interrupted if any one fuse blows.High voltage fuses are used to protect instrument transformers used for electricity metering, or for small power transformers where the expense of a circuit breaker is not necessary.

- **Resettable Fuses :** They are -called self-resetting fuses use a thermoplastic conductive element known as a Polymeric Positive Temperature Coefficient (or PPTC) thermistor that impedes the circuit during an overcurrent condition by increasing device resistance. These devices are often used in aerospace/nuclear applications where replacement is difficult, or on a computer motherboard so that a shorted mouse or keyboard does not cause motherboard damage.

Fig. 1.21 : Resettable fuse

Features

Glass cartridge and plug fuses allow direct inspection of the fusible element.

Other fuses have other indication methods including

- **Indicating Pin or Striker Pin :** extends out of the fuse cap when the element is blown.

- **Indicating Disc :** a coloured disc which is flush mounted in the end cap of the fuse falls out when the element is blown.

- **Element Window :** a small window built into the fuse body to provide visual indication of a blown element.

- **External Trip Indicator :** similar function to striker pin, but can be externally attached (using clips) to a compatible fuse.

Fuse Wire Rating : The melting point and specific resistance of different metals used for fuse wire are given in table below

Metal	Melting Point	Specific Resistance
Aluminium	240°F	2.86 µ Ω - cm
Copper	2000°F	1.72 µ Ω - cm
Lead	624°F	21.0 µ Ω - cm
Silver	1830°F	1.64 µ Ω - cm
Tin	463°F	11.3 µ Ω - cm
Zinc	787°F	6.1 µ Ω - cm

SOLVED EXAMPLES

Example 1.1 : A filament of 230V, 100w lamp is to be constructed. The temperature of filament is to be 2460°C at 100 w dissipation. Rasistivity of the filament material at 20°C is 4.3×10^{-6} Ω cm and temperature coefficient is 0.005/°C calculate the length of the filament at 20°C if its diameter at 20°C is 0.026 mm.

Solution : Given : V = 230 V, W_{diss} = 100 W, α_{20} = 0.005/°C, ρ_{20} = 4.3×10^{-6} Ω-cm,

$$d = 0.026 \text{ mm.}$$

$\therefore$ $\qquad\qquad$ r = 0.013 mm

Power dissipated $= W = I^2 R$

$\therefore$ $\qquad 100 = \left(\dfrac{V}{R}\right)^2 R = \dfrac{V^2}{R} = \dfrac{(230)^2}{R_{2460}}$

$\therefore$ $\qquad R_{2460} = 529 \ \Omega$

$$R_{2460} = R_{20} [1 + \alpha_{20} \cdot (T_2 - T_1)]$$

$\therefore$ $\qquad 529 = R_{20} [1 + 0.005 \times (2460 - 20)]$

$\therefore$ $\qquad R_{20} = \dfrac{529}{13.2} = 40.075 \ \Omega$

At 20°C,

$\therefore$ $\qquad R_{20} = \rho_{20} \left(\dfrac{l_{20}}{A_{20}}\right)$

$\therefore$ $\qquad 40.075 = 4.3 \times 10^{-6} \left(\dfrac{l_{20}}{\pi \cdot (0.013 \times 10^{-3})^2}\right)$

$\therefore$ $\qquad 40.075 = \dfrac{4.3 \times 10^{-6}}{5.309 \times 10^{-9}} \times l_{20}$

$\therefore$ $\qquad l_{20} = \dfrac{40.075 \times 5.309}{4.3}$

$\therefore$ $\qquad l_{20} = 49.48 \text{ cm}$

$\therefore$ $\qquad l_{20} = 0.4958 \text{ m}$

Example 1.2 : Annealed copper has resistivity of 1.56×10^{-8} Ω-m at 300°K. With 2 atomic percent Nickel, the resistivity of alloy of copper and Nickel becomes 4.06×10^{-8} Ω-m. With the addition of 3 atomic percent silver, the resistivity of copper and silver alloy is found to be 1.98×10^{-8} Ω-m. What will be the resistivity of copper alloy for 0.5 atomic percent of nickel and 1.2 atomic percent of silver at 300°K.

Solution : Given :

$$\rho_{Cu} = 1.56 \times 10^{-8} \ \Omega\text{-m}$$

$$\rho_{Cu\text{-}Ni} = 4.06 \times 10^{-8} \ \Omega\text{-m}$$

$$= 1.56 \times 10^{-8} + 2 \times \rho_{\text{increase per atomic percent}}$$

$$\rho_{\text{increase per atomic percent Ni}} = \frac{(4.06 - 1.56) \times 10^{-8}}{2}$$

$$= 1.25 \times 10^{-8} \ \Omega\text{-m}$$

$$\rho_{Cu\text{-}Ag} = 1.98 \times 10^{-8} + 3 \times \rho_{\text{increase per atomic percent}}$$

$$\rho_{\text{increase per atomic percent of Ag}} = \frac{(1.98 \times 1.56) \times 10^{-8}}{3}$$

$$= 0.14 \times 10^{-8} \ \Omega\text{-m}$$

$$\rho_{Cu\text{-}Ni\text{-}Ag} = 1.56 \times 10^{-8} + 0.5 \times 1.25 \times 10^{-8} + 1.2 \times 0.14 \times 10^{-8}$$

$$= 2.353 \times 10^{-8} \ \Omega\text{-m}$$

Example 1.3 : The filament of a 230 V incandescent lamp is to be drawn from a wire having a diameter of 0.025 mm and resistivity at 20°C of 4.3×10^{-6} Ω-cm. If co-efficient of temperature $\alpha = 0.05/°C$. Calculate the length of filament to dissipate 100 W at filament temperature of 2600°C.

Solution : Solution of this problem is same as numarical no. 1.

$$R_{2600°C} = 529 \ \Omega,$$

$$\rho_{2600} = 59.77 \times 10^{-6} \ \Omega\text{-cm}$$

$$I = 43.45 \ cm$$

Example 1.4 : A specimen of copper wire has resistivity of 1.6×10^{-6} Ω-cm at 0°C and a temperature coefficient of $\frac{1}{254.5}$ at 20°C. Find the resistivity and temperature co-efficient of the wire at 50°C.

Solution : Given : $\alpha_{20} = 1/254.5$ per degree, $\rho_0 = 1.6 \times 10^{-6}$, T = 50.

$$\alpha_{20} = \frac{1}{\dfrac{1}{\alpha_0} + 20} = \frac{1}{254.5}$$

$\therefore$ Resisvitity at 50°C,

$$\rho_t = \rho_0 [1 + \alpha_0 \ t]$$

$\therefore$

$$\rho_{50} = \rho_0 (1 + \alpha_0 \ 50)$$

$$= 1.6 \times 10^{-6} \left(1 + \frac{1}{234.5} \times 50 \right)$$

$$\rho_{50} = 1.941 \times 10^{-6} \ \Omega\text{-cm}$$

$$\therefore \quad \alpha_{50} = \frac{\alpha_0}{1 + \alpha_0 (50)}$$

$$= \frac{1/234.5}{1 + \dfrac{1}{234.5} (50)}$$

$$\therefore \quad \alpha_{50} = 3.515 \times 10^{-3}$$

Example 1.5 : Calculate the resistance of a wire at 50°C which is 300 m long and has an area of cross-section of 25 mm². The wire is made of aluminium. Resistivity of aluminium at 15°C is 2.7 Ω-m, temperature coefficient of aluminium is 0.004°C at 0°C.

Solution : Given : l= 300 m, a = 25 mm^2 = 25 × 10^{-6} m^2, T_2 = 50, T_1 = 15, ρ at 15°C = 2.7 Ω-m = ρ_{15}, α_0 = 0.004

$$\therefore \quad R_{15} = \rho_{15} \times \frac{l}{a}$$

$$= 2.7 \times \frac{300}{25 \times 10^{-6}}$$

$$= 32.4 \times 10^{-6} \, \Omega$$

$$R_{50} = R_{15} [1 + \alpha_{15} (T_2 - T_1)]$$

$$= 32.4 \times 10^6 \left[1 + \left(\frac{\alpha_0}{1 + \alpha_0 \, t} \right) (T_2 - T_1) \right]$$

$$= 32.4 \times 10^6 \left[1 + \left(\frac{0.004}{1 + 0.004 \times 15} \right) (50 - 15) \right]$$

$$= 32.4 \times 10^6 \left[1 + \frac{0.004 \times 35}{1 + 0.006} \right]$$

$$= 32.4 \times 10^6 \left[1 + \frac{0.14}{1.06} \right]$$

$$= 32.4 \times 10^6 [1 + 0.132]$$

$$= 32.4 \times 10^6 \times 1.132$$

$$\therefore \quad R_{50} = 36.22 \times 10^6 \, \Omega$$

Example 1.6 : A 60 W, 230V filament bulb operates at 2000°C. Room temperature is 25°C. Temperature coefficient of filament material is 4.44 × 10^{-3} /°C. Determine the length of filament at room temperature if diameter of the filament wire at room temperature is 2.546 mm. Given resistivity of filament material at 25°C is 459.55 × 10^{-6} Ω-m. Also find currents drawn by the bulb during switching and during operation at 2000°C.

Solution : Given : V = 230 V, P = 60 W, α_{25} = 4.44 × 10^{-3}, T_2 = 2000°C, T_1 = 25°C, ρ_{25} = 459.55 × 10^{-6} Ω-m, d = 2.546 mm

$$R_{2000} = \frac{(230)^2}{60} = \frac{V^2}{P}$$

$$R_{2000} = 881.67 \ \Omega$$

$$R_{2000} = R_{25} \left[1 + \alpha_{25} (T_2 - T_1) \right]$$

$$\therefore \quad 881.67 = R_{25} \left[1 + 4.44 \times 10^{-3} (1975) \right]$$

$$\therefore \quad R_{25} = 90.25 \ \Omega$$

$$\text{Area of cross-section} = a = \frac{\pi}{4} (d)^2$$

$$= \frac{\pi}{4} (2.546 \times 10^{-3})^2$$

$$\therefore \quad a = 5.092 \times 10^{-6} \ m^2$$

$$R_{25} = \rho_{25} \times \frac{l}{a}$$

$$90.25 = 459.55 \times 10^{-6} \cdot \frac{l}{5.092 \times 10^{-6}}$$

$$\therefore \quad l = \frac{459.55 \times 10^{-6}}{459.55 \times 10^{-6}} = 1 \ m$$

$$\text{Current at switching (at 25°C)} = I_{25} = \frac{V}{R_{25}}$$

$$I_{25} = \frac{230}{90.25} = 2.548 \ A$$

$$\text{Current at operation at 2000°C} = I_{2000} = \frac{V}{R_{2000}}$$

$$I_{2000} = \frac{230}{881.67} = 0.26 \ A$$

Example 1.7 : A copper conductor of resistance 80Ω at 40°C is heated upto 100°C. The temperature coefficient of resistance at 0°C is 0.00531 per degree. Calculate the resistance when the conductor is at 100°C.

Solution : Given : $T_2 = 100°C$, $T_1 = 40°C$, $R_{Cu40} = 80\Omega$

And temperature coefficient of resistance at 0°C.

$$(\alpha_0) = 0.00531 \ \text{per degree}$$

$$\therefore \quad \alpha_{40} = \frac{\alpha_0}{(1 + 40 \ \alpha_0)}$$

$$\alpha_{40} = \frac{0.00531}{1 + 40 \times 0.00531}$$

$$= 0.00437947$$

$$= 0.00438$$

$$R_{100} = R_{40} \left[1 + \alpha_{40} (100 - 40) \right]$$

$$= 80 \left[1 + 0.00438 \times 60 \right]$$

$$= 80 \times 1.2628$$

$$\therefore \qquad R_{100} = 101.024 \ \Omega$$

Example 1.8 : A 230 V filament lamp dissipate 60 watt at 2700°C. The resistivity of filament material at 20°C is 4.3×10^{-6} Ω-cm and its temperature coefficient at 20°C is 0.005/°C. Calculate the length of filament at 20°C is 20°C if its diameter at 20°C is 0.028 mm.

Solution : Given : V = 230 V, W_{diss} = 60 W, α_{20} = 0.005/°C, ρ_{20} = 4.3×10^{-6} Ω-cm, d = 0.028 mm.

$$\therefore \qquad 100 = \left(\frac{V}{R}\right)^2 R = \frac{V^2}{4} = \frac{(230)^2}{R_{2700}}$$

$$\therefore \qquad R_{2700} = 882 \ \Omega$$

$$R_{2700} = R_{20} [1 + \alpha_{20} \cdot (T_2 - T_1)]$$

$$\therefore \qquad 882 = R_{20} [1 + 0.005 \times (2700 - 20)]$$

$$\therefore \qquad R_{20} = \frac{882}{14.4} = 61.25 \ \Omega$$

At 20°C,

$$\therefore \qquad R_{20} = \rho_{20} \left(\frac{l_{20}}{A_{20}}\right)$$

$$\therefore \qquad 61.25 = 4.3 \times 10^{-6} \left[\frac{l_{20}}{\pi \cdot (0.014 \times 10^{-3})^2}\right]$$

$$\therefore \qquad 61.25 = \frac{4.3 \times 10^{-6}}{6.168 \times 10^{-9}} \times l_{20}$$

$$\therefore \qquad l_{20} = \frac{61.25 \times 6.168 \times 10^{-9}}{4.3 \times 10^{-6}}$$

$$\therefore \qquad l_{20} = 87.859 \ cm$$

$$\therefore \qquad l_{20} = 0.87859 \ m$$

Example 1.9 : Annealed copper has resistivity 17.2×10^{-9} Ωm at 20°C with 2 atomic percentage of nickel the resistivity of alloy of copper and nickel becomes 4.06×10^{-8} Ωm. With the addition of 3 percent atomic silver the resistivity of alloy of copper and silver becomes 1.98×10^{-8} Ωm. What will be the resistivity of copper alloy for addition of 0.3 atomic percent of nickel and 0.2 atomic percent of silver at 20°C.

Solution : Given :

$$\rho_{cu} = 17.2 \times 10^{-9} = 1.72 \times 10^{-8} \ \Omega m$$

$$\rho_{cu-Ni} = 4.06 \times 10^{-8}$$

$$= 1.72 \times 10^{-8} + 2 \times \rho_{increase}$$

$$\therefore \qquad \rho_{increase/atomic \ percent \ Ni} = (4.06 - 1.72) \times 10^{-8}$$

$$= 2.34 \times 10^{-8} \ \Omega m$$

$$\rho_{cu-Ag} = 1.98 \times 10^{-8}$$

$$= 1.72 \times 10^{-8} + 3 \times \rho_{increase}$$

$$\therefore \qquad \rho_{increase/atomic \ percent \ Ag} = \frac{(1.98 - 1.72) \times 10^{-8}}{3}$$

$$= 0.087 \times 10^{-8} \ \Omega m$$

$$\therefore \quad \rho_{cu\text{-}Ni\text{-}Ag} = 1.72 \times 10^{-8} + 2 \times 2.34 \times 10^{-8} + 0.087 \times 10^{-8} \times 0.2$$

$$= (1.72 + 4.68 + 0.0174) \times 10^{-8}$$

$$= 6.4174 \times 10^{-8} \ \Omega m$$

Example 1.10 : Annealed copper has resistivity of 1.56×10^{-8} Ωm at 300°K with 2 atomic percent nickel, the resistivity of alloy of copper and nickel becomes 4.06×10^{-8} Ωm. With the addition of 3 atomic percent silver the resistivity of copper and silver alloy as found to be 1.98×10^{-8} Ωm. What will be the resistivity of copper alloy for 0.2 atomic percent of nickel and 0.4 atomic percent of silver at 300°K.

Solution : Given :

$$\rho_{cu} = 1.56 \times 10^{-8} \ \Omega m$$

$$\rho_{cu\text{-}Ni} = 4.06 \times 10^{-8}$$

$$= 1.56 \times 10^{-8} + 2 \times \rho_{increase}$$

$$\therefore \quad \rho_{increase/atomic\ percent\ Ni} = (4.06 - 1.56) \times 10^{-8}$$

$$= 1.25 \times 10^{-8} \ \Omega m$$

$$\rho_{cu\text{-}Ag} = 1.98 \times 10^{-8}$$

$$= 1.56 \times 10^{-8} + 3 \times \rho_{increase}$$

$$\therefore \quad \rho_{increase/atomic\ percent\ Ag} = \frac{(1.98 - 1.56) \times 10^{-8}}{3}$$

$$= 0.14 \times 10^{-8} \ \Omega m$$

$$\therefore \quad \rho_{cu\text{-}Ni\text{-}Ag} = 1.56 \times 10^{-8} + 2 \times 1.25 \times 10^{-8} + 0.14 \times 10^{-8} \times 0.4$$

$$= 1.866 \times 10^{-8} \ \Omega m$$

Example 1.11 : The resistivity of copper at 300°K is 1.56×10^{-8} Ωm. With 2 atomic percent Nickel, the resistivity of copper and nickel becomes 4.06×10^{-8} Ωm at 300°K with 0.2 atomic percent of Nickel and 0.4 at atomic percent of silver at 300°K the resistivity becomes 1.866×10^{-8} Ωm. What will be the resistivity of Cu-silver alloy at 300°K with 3 atomic percent of silver?

Solution : Given :

$$\rho_{cu} = 1.56 \times 10^{-8} \ \Omega m$$

$$\rho_{cu\text{-}Ni} = 4.06 \times 10^{-8} \ \Omega m$$

$$= 1.56 \times 10^{-8} + 2 \ \rho_{increase}$$

$$\therefore \quad \rho_{increase/atomic\ percent\ Ni} = (4.06 - 1.56) \times 10^{-8}$$

$$= 1.25 \times 10^{-8} \ \Omega m$$

$$\rho_{cu\text{-}Ag} = 1.866 \times 10^{-8}$$

$$= 1.56 \times 10^{-8} + 4 \times \rho_{increase}$$

$$\therefore \quad \rho_{increase/atomic\ percent\ Ag} = \frac{(1.866 - 1.56) \times 10^{-8}}{3}$$

$$= 0.306 \times 10^{-8} \ \Omega m$$

$$\therefore \quad \rho_{cu\text{-}Ni\text{-}Ag} = 1.56 \times 10^{-8} + 2 \times 1.25 \times 10^{-8} + 0.306 \times 10^{-8} \times 0.4$$

$$= (1.56 + 2.5 + 0.1224) \times 10^{-8}$$

$$= 4.1824 \times 10^{-8} \ \Omega m$$

Example 1.12 : Calculate the length of heater element having 0.4 mm diameter to get a resistance of 40Ω and 1000 watts if

(a) Nichrome wire having resistivity 100×10^{-8} Ωm is used.

(b) Copper wire having resistivity 1.72 10^{-8} Ωm is used. Which wire will you prefer for heater element?

Solution : Given : $R_{cu} = 40\Omega, d = 0.4$ mm

$$a = \frac{\pi}{4} d^2$$

$$= \frac{\pi}{4} \times (0.4 \times 10^{-3})^2$$

$$= 1.2566 \times 10^{-7}$$

$$R_{cu} = \frac{\rho \, l_{cu}}{a}$$

$$l_{cu} = \frac{R_{cu} \cdot a}{\rho}$$

$$= \frac{40 \times 1.2566 \times 10^{-7}}{1.72 \times 10^{-8}}$$

$$\therefore \qquad l_{cu} = 292.24 \text{ m}$$

So length of copper heater element required is 292.24 m

$$R_{Ni} = \frac{\rho \, l_{Ni}}{a}$$

$$\therefore \qquad l_{Ni} = \frac{R_{Ni} \cdot a}{\rho}$$

$$= \frac{40 \times 1.2566 \times 10^{-7}}{100 \times 10^{-8}}$$

$$\therefore \qquad l_{Ni} = 5.0264 \text{ m}$$

So, length of nichrome heater element required is 5.0264 m. Hence, nichrome heater element is preferred than copper element.

Example 1.13 : Annealed copper has resistivity of 1.56×10^{-8} Ωm at 300°K. With 4 atomic percent nickel, the resistivity of copper and nickel becomes 4.06×10^{-8} Ωm. With the addition of 3 atomic percent silver the resistivity of copper and silver alloy is found to be 2.10×10^{-8} Ωm. What will be resistivity of copper alloy for 0.8 atomic percent of nickel and 1.5 atomic percent of silver at 300°K?

Solution : Given :

$$\rho_{cu} = 1.56 \times 108 \text{ } \Omega m$$

$$\rho_{cu \cdot Ni} = 4.06 \times 10^{-8}$$

$$= 1.56 \times 10^{-8} + 4 \cdot \rho_{increase}$$

$$\rho_{increase} / \text{atomic \% age of Ni} = \frac{(4.06 - 1.56) \times 10^{-8}}{4}$$

$$= 0.625 \times 10^{-8} \text{ } \Omega m$$

$$\rho_{cu \cdot Ag} = 2.10 \times 10^{-8} + 3 \times \rho_{increase} \text{ per atomic percentage}$$

$$\therefore \rho_{increase} \text{ per atomic percentage of Ag} = \frac{(2.10 - 1.56) \times 10^{-8}}{3}$$

$$= 0.18 \times 10^{-8} \ \Omega m$$

$$\rho_{cu \cdot Ni-Ag} = 1.56 \times 10^{-8} + 0.8 \times 0.625 \times 10^{-8} + 1.5 \times 0.18 \times 10^{-8}$$

$$= 2.33 \times 10^{-8} \ \Omega m$$

Example 1.14 : A copper conductor has resistance of 80Ω at $40°C$. It is heated to $100°C$. Calculate its resistance and temperature coefficient of resistance at $100°C$. Given $\alpha_0 = 0.00531$ per degree centigrade.

Solution :

$$\alpha_{40} = \frac{\alpha_0}{1 + 40 \ \alpha_0}$$

$$\alpha_{40} = 0.00438 \ /°C$$

$$R_{100} = R_{40} [1 + \alpha_{40} (100 - 40)]$$

$$\therefore \quad R_{100} = 101.024 \ \Omega$$

$$\alpha_{100} = \frac{a_0}{1 + 100 \ (a_0)}$$

$$\alpha_{100} = 0.00346 \ /°C$$

Example 1.15 : A filament of a 230V, 60 W lamp is to be constructed. The temperature of the filament is to be $1500°C$ at 60 W. Resistivity of the filament material at $30°C$ is $5.3 \times 10^{-6} \ \Omega$-cm and temperature co-efficient $\alpha_{30} = 0.005/°C$. Calculate the length of the filament at $30°C$ if its diameter at $30°C$ is 0.025 mm.

Solution : Given : V = 230, W_{diss} = 60 W, $\alpha_{30} = 0.005/°C$, $\rho_{30} = 5.3 \times 10^{-6}$, d = 0.025 mm, r = 0.0125 mm

$$\text{Power dissipated} = W = I^2R$$

$$60 = \left(\frac{V}{R}\right)^2 R$$

$$= \frac{V^2}{R}$$

$$= \frac{(230)^2}{R_{1500}}$$

$$\therefore \quad R_{1500} = 881.7 \ \Omega$$

$\therefore$ $\qquad$ $R_{1500} = R_{30} [1 + \alpha_{30} (T_2 - T_1)]$

$\therefore$ $\qquad$ $881.7 = R_{30} [1 + 0.005 (1500 - 30)]$

$\therefore$ $\qquad$ $881.7 = R_{30} [1 + 7.35]$

$$R_{30} = \frac{881.7}{8.35} = 105.6 \ \Omega$$

At 30°C,

$$R_{30} = \rho_{30} \left(\frac{l_{30}}{A_{30}}\right)$$

$$105.6 = 5.3 \times 10^{-6} \left(\frac{l_{30}}{r(0.0125 \times 10^{-3})^2}\right)$$

$$105.6 = \frac{5.3 \times 10^{-6}}{1.5625 \times 10^{-10} \times l_{30}}$$

$$105.6 = 3.392 \times 10^{-4} \times l_{30}$$

$\therefore$ $\qquad$ $$l_{30} = \frac{105.6}{3.392 \times 10^4}$$

$$= 31.132 \times 10^{-4}$$

$$= 3.1132 \times 10^{-3}$$

$\therefore$ $\qquad$ $l_{30} = 3.1132 \ mm$

QUESTIONS

1. Explain properties of conducting materials.

2. Explain classification of thermocouples.

3. Explain materials use for element filament lamp.

4. What is bi-metal?

5. Short note on

    (i)   Silver alloys   (ii) Eureka

    (iii) Bronze   (iv) Constantan

6. Explain the factors which affect the resistivity of conducting material. Give examples in support of your answer.

7.   What is thermal bimetal? Name some bimetals and their applications.

8.   Give the electrical properties and applications of the following materials

   (i)   Aluminium

   (ii)   Carbon

   (iii) Nichrome

   (iv)   Eureka

9.   Give the salient properties and applications of high conductive and high resistivity materials.

10. Why is carbon preferred for brushes in electric machines?

11. State properties and application of

   (i) Eureka

   (ii) Tungsten

12. What properties of conductors are required for electric machines? Discuss the conductors required for D.C. machines.

13. Explain the factors which affect the resistivity of conducting material. Give examples in support of your answer.

14. Describe the properties and applications of the following materials

   (i)   Constantan

   (ii)   Nichrome

   (iii) Canthal

   (iv)   Bronze

15. What are thermocouples? Name some thermocouples and their applications.

16. Describe the groups into which the materials as electric conductors are divided.

17. Why is carbon preferred for brushes in electric machines?

18. List the properties of a conductive material. Describe in brief the properties, characteristics and application of aluminum as a conductive material.

19. State the properties and application of

   (a) Eureka   (b) Tungsten   (c) Kanthal

20. Why is carbon preferred for brushes in electric machines?

21. What are the groups into which solders are grouped? Give their applications.

22. A 230 V filament lamp dissipates 60 Watt at 2700°C. Resistivity of filament material at 20°C is 4.3×10^{-6} Ω-cm and its temperature coefficient at 20°C is 0.005/°C. Calculate the length of filament at 20°C if its diameter at 20°C if its diameter at 20°C is 0.028 mm.

23. Annealed copper has resistivity 17.2×10^{-9} Ωm at 20°C. With 2 atomic percent of nickel, the resistivity of alloy of copper and nickel becomes 4.06×10^{-8} Ωm. With the addition of 3 percent atomic silver, the resistivity of alloy of copper and silver becomes 1.98×10^{-8} Ωm. What will be the resistivity of copper alloy for addition of 0.3 atomic percent of nickel and 0.2 atomic percent of silver at 20°C?

24. What is a bi-metal? Give two applications of bi-metals.

25. State properties and applications of

    (a) Nichrome   (b) Constantan

26. Describe the groups into which the materials as electric conductors are divided?

27. Name the materials used in the following cases with reasons.

    (a) Element in filament lamp.

    (b) Resistance in loading rheostat.

28. Calculate the length of heater element having 0.4 mm diameter to get a resistance of 40 Ω and 1000 Watts if

    (a) Nichrome wire having resistivity 100×10^{-8} Ωm is used.

    (b) Copper wire having resistivity 1.72×10^{-8} Ωm is used. Which wire will you prefer for heater element?

29. Write down properties and applications of constantan, nickel-chromium alloy, tungsten, Kanthal, silver, copper alloy and carbon.

30. Describe lamp filament, solders, thermal bi-metal and thermocouple.

31. State the properties and applications of

    1. Nichrome

    2. Manganin

    3. Tungsten

32. Explain the factors which affect resistivity of conducting materials.

33. What are thermocouples? Name some thermocouples. Give their applications.

34. Annealed copper has resistivity of 1.56×10^{-8} Ωm at 300°K. With 4 atomic percent nickel, the resistivity of copper and nickel becomes 4.06×10^{-8} Ωm. With the addition of 3 atomic percent silver the resistivity of copper the silver alloy is found to be 2.10×10^{-8} Ωm. What will be resistivity of copper alloy for 0.8 atomic percent of nickel and 1.5 atomic percent of silver at 300°K?

35. A copper conductor has resistance of 80 Ω at 40°C. It is heated to 100°C. Calculate its resistance and temperature coefficient of resistance at 100°C. Given α_0 = 0.00531 per degree centigrade.

36. State the properties and applications of

    (i)   Tungsten   (ii) Eureka

    (iii) Kanthal   (iv) Nichrome

37. Why is carbon preferred for brushes in electric machines?

38. What are the groups into which solders are grouped? Give their applications.

39. Describe in brief the properties and applications of aluminium as conductive material.

40. Write a short note on "Thermocouples".

41. State properties and applications of

    (i)   Eureka   (ii) Nichrome

    (iii) ACSR   (iv) Carbon

42. A copper conductor of resistance 80 Ω at 40°C is heated upto 100°C. The temperature coefficient of resistance at 0°C is 0.00531 per degree. Calculate the resistance when the conductor is at 100°C.

43. Why is carbon preferred for brushes in electric machines?

44. What are thermocouple? Name some thermocouples and their applications.

45. A filament of a 230 V, 100 W lamp is to be constructed. The temperature of the filament is to be 2460°C at 100 W dissipation. Resistivity of the filament material at 20°C is 4.3×10^{-6} Ωcm and temperature coefficient $\rho20$ = 0.005/°C. Calculate the length of the filament at 20°C. If its diameter at 20°C is 0.026 mm.

46. Write a short note on thermocouple.

47. What is a bi-metal? Give two applications of bimetal.

48. Write a short note on superconductivity.

49. Give the electrical properties and applications of Nichrome and Tungsten.

50. A filament of a 230 V, 60 W lamp is to be constructed. The temperature of the filament is to be 1500°C at 60 W. Resistivity of the filament material at 30°C is 5.3×10^{-6} Ω-cm and temperature co-efficient α_{30} = 0.005/°C. Calculate the length of the filament at 30°C if its diameter at 30°C is 0.025 mm.

51. Describe the groups into which the materials as electric conductors are divided.

✠ ✠ ✠

INSULATING MATERIALS

2.1 INTRODUCTION

Most substances fall into one of two classes: conductor or insulator. Conductors permit the passage of charge or heat through them, while insulators do not. Associated with the atoms of materials, there is an outer band of electrons called the valence band apart from conduction and insulation bond. When these outer valence electrons can easily become detached from the nucleus and can move freely, the material is said to be a conductor. in an insulator, there are no, or at most very few, free electrons. The actual conductance happens when the electrons change energy levels, or move from one valence band to another. If there are no nearby empty levels, then the electron will not be able to gain any energy and the material behaves like an insulator. These materials have very high resistivity i.e. offers a very high resistance to the flow of electric current. Insulating materials plays an important part in various electrical and electronic circuits. In domestic wiring, insulating material protect us from shock and also prevent leakage current to flow.

Resistivity

Resistivity is the resistance between the two opposite faces of a cube having each side equal to one meter. Resistivity of conductors is 10^{-8} to 10^{-3} ohm-m, insulators is 10^{10-20} ohm-m, semiconductors is $100^{-0.5}$ ohm-m. So, insulating material offers a wide range of uses in various engineering applications.

Factors Affecting Selection of an Insulating Material

- **Operating Condition :** Before selecting an insulating material for a particular application the selection should be made on the basis of operating temperature, magnitude of voltage and current and pressure.

- **Easy in Shaping :** Shape and size is also important affect.

- **Availability of Material :** The material is easily available.

- **Cost :** Cost is also a important factor.

  Knowledge of various types of insulating materials is the most powerful tool in selection of right insulating material for proper use.

2.2 PROPERTIES OF INSULATING MATERIALS

- Electrical properties
- Thermal properties
- Chemical properties
- Physical/Mechanical properties

2.2.1 Electrical Properties

- Insulation resistance or resistivity
- Dielectric strength or breakdown voltage
- Dielectric constant
- Dielectric loss

Insulation Resistance

The resistance offered to the flow of electric current through the material is called insulation resistance. Insulation resistance is of two types

- Volume insulation resistance.
- Surface insulation resistance.

Volume Resistance and Resistivity

The resistance offered to current I_v which flows through the material is called volume insulation resistance. For a cube of unit dimensions this is called volume resistivity. As shown in Fig. 2.1 from A to C.

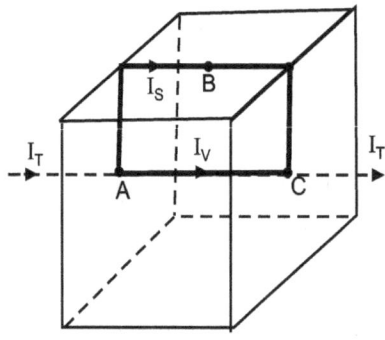

Fig. 2.1

Surface Resistance

The resistance offered to current which flows over the surface of the insulating material is called surface insulation resistance. As from A to B and then B to C as shown in Fig. 2.1.

Factors affecting insulation resistance

- Temperature
- Moisture
- Applied voltage
- Ageing

Temperature

As the temperature of the insulating material rises its insulation resistance keeps on falling.

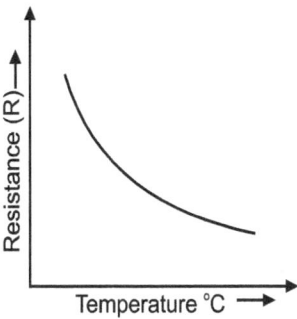

Fig. 2.2

Moisture

Insulation resistance is reduced if the material absorbs moisture, so insulation material should be non-hygroscopic.

Applied Voltage

Applied voltage also affects insulation resistance.

Dielectric Strength

Dielectric strength is the minimum voltage which when applied to an insulating material will result in the destruction of its insulating properties.

Ageing

Ageing reduces the insulation resistance. As age of insulation material is increased the insulation resistance decreases.

2.2.2 Thermal Properties

- Heat resistance
- Permissible temperature rise
- Effect of overloading on the life of an electrical appliance
- Thermal conductivity

Heat Resistance

This is general property of insulating material to withstand temperature variation within desirable limits, without damaging its other important properties.

If an insulator has constructive properties at ambient temperature but, if it is not able to retain these, then it is not a good insulator. The insulator which is capable of withstanding higher temperature without deterioration of its other properties can be used for operation for such higher temperature.

Classification on the Basis of Operating Temperature

Class 'Y' Insulation : Material if un-impregnated fall in this category with operating temperature up to 90°C. e.g. paper, cardboard, cotton, poly vinyl chloride etc.

Class 'A' Insulation : Insulators of class Y when impregnated fall in class A with operating temperature of about 105°C.

Class 'E' Insulation : Insulation of this class has operating temperature of 120°C. Insulators used for enameling of wires fall in this category e.g. PVC etc.

Class 'B' Insulation : Impregnated materials fall in class B insulation category with operating temperatures of about 130°C e.g. impregnated mica, asbestos, fiber glass etc.

Class 'F' Insulation : Impregnated materials, impregnated or glued with better varnishes e.g. polyurethane, epoxides etc. fall in this category with operating temperature of about 155°C.

Class 'H' Insulation : Insulating materials either impregnated or not, operating at 180°C falls in this category e.g. fiber glass, mica, asbestos, silicon rubber etc.

Class 'C' Insulation : Insulators which have operating temperatures more than 180°C falls in class C insulation category e.g. glass, ceramics, poly terafluoro ethylene, mica etc.

Permissible Temperature

There is always some recommended operating temperature for an insulator. The operating temperature has a bearing on the life of the concerned apparatus. A thumb rule suggested by many experts is that life of insulator is halved for 8-10 degree centigrade rise above the recommended operating temperature for a given apparatus.

2.2.3 Chemical Properties

- Solubility
- Chemical resistance
- Weather ability

Solubility : In certain application insulation can be applied only after it is dissolved in some solvents. In such cases, the insulating material should be soluble in certain appropriate solvent. If the insulating material is soluble in water then moisture in the atmosphere will always be able to remove the applied insulation and cause break down of material.

Chemical Resistance : Presence of gases, water, acids, alkalis and salts affects different insulators differently, Chemically, a material is a better insulator if it resists chemical action.

Certain plastic are found approaching this condition. thus, their use is very much increase.

Weatherability : Insulators come in contact with atmosphere both during manufacture or operation. The contact of insulation with atmosphere is often so complete that even the less chemically aggressive atmosphere can prove a threat to the smooth running of apparatus.

Hygroscopicity : The property of insulating material by virtue of which it absorbs moisture. The insulating material should be non-hygroscopic. The absorption of moisture reduces the resistivity of the insulator.

2.2.4 Physical/Mechanical Properties

- Mechanical strength
- Porosity
- Machiability and mouldability
- Density
- Brittleness

Mechanical Strength : The insulating material should have high mechanical strength to bear the mechanical stresses and strains during operation.

Temperature and humidity are the main factors which reduce the mechanical strength of insulating materials.

Porosity : A material having very small holes in it is called as a porous material. Insulator absorbs moisture if it is porous, which results in reducing its resistivity as will as mechanical strength. Porous materials are impregnated with varnishes or resins to fill their pores which make them non-porous thus better insulating materials.

Machiability and Mouldability : This property of insulating material helps us to give the desired shapes to the insulating materials.

Density : The insulating material should have low density to reduce the weight of equipment in which that insulating material is being used.

Brittleness : The insulating material should not be brittle. Otherwise insulators may fracture easily due to stresses.

2.3 INSULATING MATERIALS AND THEIR APPLICATIONS

There are thousand of insulating materials available in the market. Insulation technology is one of those few branches where the numbers of materials available for a particular application are more than one. Any special requirement can be served by some special material.

Selection of an Insulating Material

- **Operating Condition :** Operating temperature, pressure, operating voltage and current are to be considered for the selection of a particular material.
- **Easy to Shape :** For ease of fabrication of equipment the material should be easy to shape.
- **Availability :** Material should be easily available.
- **Cost :** For cost-effectiveness of the insulating products the material should not have a very high cost compared to the other options available for the same use.

(1) Mica and Mica Products

Mica is an inorganic mineral. It is one of the best natural insulating materials available.

It is one of the oldest insulating materials of out-standing performance. India fortunately claims the biggest reserves of mica in world.

About 80% of total World requirement of mica for electrical industry is furnished by India.

Chief sources of supply are India, Brazil and U.S.A. But the best quality is available in India. The basic composition is $KH_2Al_3(SiO_4)_3$.

Properties

- Strong, tough and less flexible
- Colorless, Yellow, Silver or Green
- Very good Insulating properties
- High resistance also High chemical Resistance
- Not affected by alkalis
- Specific Gravity : 2.6 to 3.6 g/cc
- Operating Temperature : 600°C
- Resistivity : 10^{15-16} ohm-m
- Dielectric Strength : 75 to 80 kV/mm

Applications

- Capacitor
- Commutators of DC machines
- Electric irons
- Electric hot plates
- Electric toasters.

(a) Glass Bonded Mica

Ground mica and powdered glass when molded makes glass bonded mica. The ratio of mica and glass is 40/60 to 60/40 range.

Properties

- Highly water resistant
- Chemically stable
- Low dielectric loss
- High dielectric strength
- Moldable

Applications

- Capacitors
- The material finds its use in high humidity and high ambient temperature atmospheres.

(b) Synthetic Mica

The development of synthetic mica took place during world war II.

Although synthetic mica possesses many technical defects of natural mica.

Properties

- Operating Temperature : 1200°C
- Dielectric constant : 6 to 7
- Resistivity : 10^{15-16} ohm-m
- Low-Hygroscopicity
- Low chemical resistance

Applications

Insulation for armature and field coils mainly.

(c) Manufactured Mica

When mica flakes are held together with adhesive the product is called mica plate. The binding material is about 20%. The binding materials are shellac, epoxy and silicon resins etc.

Applications

- Commutators of DC motors and generators.
- Insulation for armature and field coils.
- Heating appliances.
- Transformers.

(d) Micanite

Very thin mica sheet bound together with adhesives are called micanites.

Applications

Commutators of DC motors and generators.

(2) Asbestos

Found in veins of serpentine rocks hence the name Serpentine asbestos. Principal sources of supply are Canada and Africa.

- (i) It is found in Cuddappah district of Andhra Pradesh in India.
- (ii) It is inorganic fibrous material.
- (iii) It is neither mechanically strong nor flexible.
- (iv) It withstands high temperature of about 400°C so used in electrical equipment as insulator.
- (v) Its dielectric strength is 3 to 4.5 kV/mm thickness.

Properties

- Specific Gravity : 1.9 to 2.7 g/cc.
- Melting Point : 1500°C
- Dielectric Strength : very High
- Hygroscopic
- Bad conductor of heat.

Applications

- It is used in low voltage work in the form of pipe, tape, cloth and board.
- Coil winding and insulating end turns.
- Arc barriers in circuit breakers and switches.
- Transformers

Industrial Asbestos Products

Asbestos use most because of its utility in engineering applications because of crystalline structure and structural stability at high temperature. However it has limitation because of low tensile strength, high dielectric loss and sensitivity towards moisture. Some of the asbestos are as follows :

(a) Asbestos Roving

Asbestos fibers reinforced with cotton or synthetic organic fibers make asbestos roving.

Applications

It finds use in insulation of cables and conductors and in heating devices.

(b) Asbestos Paper and Board

In actual use asbestos paper is further reinforced with cotton or synthetic fiber or glass fiber.

Applications

- Wrapping material in cables.
- Layer insulation in transformers.

(c) Asbestos Cement

- About 20% asbestos fiber and 80% Portland cement are the main constituents of asbestos cement. Impregnated asbestos cement products are used to overcome its hygroscopic nature.

Properties

- Good mechanical strength.
- High thermal stability.
- Excellent resistance to electrical arcing.
- Hygroscopic

Applications

These cements find their use in switch panel construction and in arcing devices.

(3) Ceramics Materials

Ceramics are materials made by high temperature firing treatment of natural clay and certain organic matters. Structurally ceramics are crystals bonded together. Other materials used with clay in different type of ceramics are Quartz, Talc, and Magnetite etc.

Properties

- Hard, strong and dense.
- Not affected by chemical action stronger in compression than tension.
- Stability at high temperatures
- Excellent dielectric properties.
- Weak in impact strength.

Applications

- Porcelain insulators
- Line insulators.

(a) Alumina

Aluminium oxide is Al_2O_3 is known as alumina.

Properties

- Specific Gravity : 3.2 to 4.2 g/cc
- Operating Temperature : 1800 °C
- Dielectric constant : 8 to 9.5
- Resistivity : 10^{14-16} ohm-m
- Low-Hygroscopicity
- High chemical resistance
- High tensile strength.

Applications

- Circuit Breakers
- Spark Plugs
- Resistor Cores
- Substrates for ICs and Power Transistors

(b) Porcelain

Porcelain are basically clays and quartz embedded in glass matrix. it used as insulators after glazing is done i.e. a thin layer of glass is glazed over the insulator.

Properties

- Specific Gravity : 2.35 to 5 g/cc
- Operating Temperature : 1200°C
- Dielectric constant : 5 to 7
- Resistivity : $10^{11\text{-}14}$ ohm-m
- Low-Hygroscopicity
- High chemical Resistance
- High tensile strength

Applications

- Transformer bushings
- Line Insulators
- Switches/ Plugs/ sockets/ Fuse Holders

(4) Steatite

It is basically a mixture of clay and talc i.e. it contains hydrous oxides of magnesium and silicon.

Properties

- Specific Gravity : 2.5 to 2.9 g/cc
- Operating Temperature : 1200 °C
- Dielectric constant : 5.7 to 6.5
- Resistivity : $10^{12\text{-}15}$ ohm-m
- Low-Hygroscopicity
- High chemical Resistance
- High tensile strength

Applications

Insulators for High frequency and high thermal shocks.

(5) Glass

It is normally transparent, brittle and hard. It is insoluble in water and the organic solvents. Glass find its use in electrical industry because of its low dielectric loss, slow aging and good mechanical strength. Glass has its limitations because it is not easy to manufacture and is dense and heavy.

Applications

- Molded devices such as electrical bushings, fuse bodies, insulators
- Capacitor
- Radio and television tubes
- Laminated boards
- Lamps/ Fluorescent Tubes

(6) Epoxy Glass

Insulating material manufactured by bonding multiple layers of glass fibre impregnated with epoxy resins is called epoxy glass.

Properties

- Dielectric constant : 5
- Resistivity : 10^{14} ohm-m
- Dielectric Strength : 0.4 kV/mm
- Non-Hygroscopic
- High chemical resistance

Applications

- Base material in printed circuit boards.
- Cases and terminal posts for instruments.

(7) Silicon Grease

Silicon grease is the fluid of silicon oxygen chains with methyl groups. It can be used over a wide range of temperatures.

Properties

- Operating Temperature : 60 to 200 °C
- Dielectric constant : 2.6
- Resistivity : High
- Non-Hygroscopic

Applications

- Capacitors
- Transformers
- In manufacturing of silicon rubber

(8) Dry Paper

The source of dry paper is cellulose obtained mainly from wood. It is obtained by pulping the wood first and then passing it through the rollers to give it the final shape.

Properties

- Resistivity : $10^{5\text{-}10}$ ohm-m
- High hygroscopicity
- Highly inflammable

Applications

It has very limited use as in Telephone cables and Small transformers

Impregnated Paper

To improve the properties of dry paper it is impregnated with oils or varnishes.

Properties

It has better properties then the dry paper in terms of mechanical strength, chemical resistance, dielectric constant, operating temperature, hygroscopicity and dielectric loss.

Applications

Underground Cables (200 to 400 V) Capacitors.

(9) Varnishes

Varnishes are obtained by dissolving the materials in oil or alcohol. They are used mainly for impregnation, surface coating and as adhesives.

Properties

- Transparent
- Non-Hygroscopic.

Applications

- Surface coating on windings
- Impregnation of paper, cotton.

(10) Rubber

Natural rubber is obtained from the milky sap of trees. It finds limited applications in the field of engineering. The reasons are rubber is a material which is stretchable to more than twice its original length without deformation.

(a) Natural Rubber

Natural rubber is extracted from the milky sap from rubber trees.

Applications

- It finds limited use in covering wires, conductors etc. for low voltage operations.
- Gloves, rubber shoes.

(b) Hard Rubber

Increased sulphur contents and extended vulcanization treatment gives rigid rubber product.

Properties

- Good electrical properties
- High tensile strength.
- Maximum permissible operating temperature is 60°C.
- Continued exposure to sun is harmful.

Applications

- Construction of storage battery housings.
- Panel boards.
- Bushings of various types etc.

2.3.1 Fibrous Insulating Materials

- Many of them are derived from cellulose which is main constituent of vegetable plants.
- It consists of elongated particles called fibres.
- The fibres are mechanically strong and cheaper. But they are Hygroscopic. Hence they are impregnated.
- Impregnation : It is a process of treating fibrous material with insulating material such as varnishes, resins, oil etc.

Advantages of Impregnation

- It reduces hygroscopic nature in materials.
- It helps in filling voids or air pockets in materials and makes them denser (more homogenous).
- It increases mechanical strength, chemical stability and ability to withstand high temperature.
- It also reduces chemical and thermal deterioration.
- Examples of fibrous insulating materials are wood, paper pressboard, asbestos, cotton, silk etc.

(1) Wood

Properties

- Cheaper.
- Easily available.
- Tensile strength depends on type of wood and it is between 700 to 1200 kg/cm^2.
- Dielectric constant varies from 2.5 to 7.7.
- However it is very hygroscopic and hence loses its mechanical properties after absorbing moisture so needs impregnation.

Applications

- It is used for slots wedges in motor and generator winding.
- It is used for making switch boards, terminal boxes, round blocks.
- It is used as a spacer between HV and LV winding in transformer.

(2) Paper

Properties

- It is easily available and cheaper.
- It can be easily wrapped around the conductor.
- Ability to withstand high temperature.
- Low dielectric loss, density has greater influence on it.
- Its dielectric strength is 4 to 10 kV/mm thickness.
- Paper is made from glass or cellulose or asbestos.

- The base materials for manufacturing insulating paper is coniferous wood.
- However its major disadvantage is that it is hygroscopic. So to improve electrical properties it is impregnated with mineral oils, varnishes etc.
- It has good mechanical strength.
- It has permittivity 2 to 3.
- It is inflammable.
- Hygroscopic.
- Resistivities $10^{5\text{-}10}$ Ωm.

(3) Pressboard

- It is less flexible as compared to paper but more mechanical strength.
- It is similar to paper but is more thicker and denser than paper.
- Its insulation resistance is 10^7 Ωm.
- Its dielectric strength is 50 kV/mm.
- Less hygroscopic than the paper.

Applications

- For making slot lining.
- As separator in transformer winding.
- It is used for making slot wedges for stator and rotor core stacks.

Two important types of pressboard (used in slot lining)

a. Pressphan

- It is hygroscopic so needs impregnation.
- It withstands maximum voltage of 600 V.
- It has good mechanical and dielectric properties.

b. Leatheroid

- It is hygroscopic so needs impregnation.
- It is thicker than pressphan.
- It is strong, tough and flexible.
- It is used for low voltages only.

(4) Cotton

Properties

- It is hygroscopic (absorbs moisture quickly).
- It has low dielectric strength.
- It can withstand temperature of 100°C.
- It is made in form of cloth or fibre and tapes.

- Its properties can be improved by impregnating it with varnish.
- Inflammable.
- Density has greater influence on dielectric strength and loss.
- Permittivity is 2 to 3.

Applications

- Cotton covered wire is widely used for winding of small and medium size machine, transformer coils.
- Chokes.
- Winding of small magnet coil etc.

(5) Silk

- It is more expensive than cotton.
- It is very thin and mechanically strong.
- It is less hygroscopic, than cotton but like cotton it requires impregnation.
- It has higher dielectric strength than cotton.
- It has better space factor than cotton.
- Its thermal conductivity is low.
- Its operating temperature is 100°C.

Applications

Since it takes less space so used for windings in fractional horse power machines.

2.3.2 Insulating Resins (Polymers)

- These are organic substances of higher molecular weight.
- These can be formed into desired shape during or after manufacture.

(a) Natural Resins :

- These are derived from plant and animal sources.
- Simple purification or slight chemical modifications is made in natural resins so that it can be used as electrical insulation.

Different types of natural resins are

(1) Amber

- It is fossil resin.
- It is light yellow in colour.
- Its specific gravity is 1.05 to 1.1.
- It has high electrical resistance.

Applications

It is mainly used to make electrical insulating components in measuring instruments.

(2) Wood Resin

- It is gummy and sticky like material.

- Its dielectric constant is 2.5 to 3.

- Its dielectric strength is 10 to 16 kV/mm.

Applications

It is used for preparation of paints and varnishes, insulating oils.

(3) Shellac

- It is natural resin, obtained from tropical trees and animals.

- It has high adhesive property.

- It has less mechanical strength.

- It has poor resistance to heat, moisture and solvents.

- Dielectric constant is 3.5.

- Its dielectric strength is 14 to 50 kV/mm.

Applications

It is used for impregnation and manufacture of micanite.

(b) Synthetic Resins

- They are also called plastics.

- Now-a-days more than 50% insulating material used are from this category.

- These are organic substances which resemble to natural resins in properties like heat resistance, plasticity.

- Its chemical composition is different from natural resins.

- These are obtained by following two methods.

1. Linear Polymerisation

- It is a chemical reaction in which the reacting materials combine with each other without producing any by-product. Thus here high molecular compound is obtained from low molecular compound. This chemical reaction takes place under the influence of elevated temperature and pressure.

2. Condensation Polymerization

- This is irreversible chemical reaction between low molecular weight compounds and produces hydrogen (H_2), hydrogen chloride (HCl), as a by-product.

- Example of this polymer is polyester.

It has the following two types

(c) Thermoplastic Resins : These are the resins which soften and melt on heating and again solidify when they are cooled. Different types of thermoplastic resins are

1. **Perspex :** It is used in model making and decoration purpose.

2. **Polyethylene**

- It is also known as polythene.

- It is obtained from polymerization of ethylene.

- It is moisture resistant. It is not soluble in many solvents except benzene and petroleum at high temperature.

- Its melting point is low and it possess good electrical and mechanical properties.

Applications

It is used for insulation of wires, high frequency cables, and television and communication cables.

3. **PVC (Poly Vinyl Chloride)**

- It is obtained by polymerization of ethylene dichloride and sodium hydroxide in the presence of catalyst at 50°C.

- Its properties can be improved by adding fillers like cotton, asbestos, powdered mica, stabilizers such as HCl, metal soap, calcium oxide.

Properties of PVC

- Resist flame and sunlight.

- High resistance to chemical action.

- More flexible.

- Non-hygroscopic.

- Low weight and reduced size.

Applications

It is used for cable insulation, insulation of wires, conduit pipes, insulation for dry batteries.

(d) Poly-Tera-Fluoro-Ethylene : It is also called Teflon. It is obtained by catalytic polymerization of tetra fluoro-ethylene.

Properties

- Good mechanical, thermal and electrical proeperties.

- Insulation resistance is very high.

- It withstands high temperature (upto 300°C).

- Water resistant.

- Specific gravity 2.1 to 2.3.
- Dielectric strength is 16 to 20 kV/m.
- Dielectric constant is 2 to 2.2.

Applications

- Used as covering for conductors and cables.
- Used as dielectric material in capacitor.

1. Thermosetting Resins

- They can not be softened by heating.
- They undergo chemical changes when moulded.
- Different types of thermosetting resins are
  - i. Bakelite
  - ii. Silicon resin
  - iii. Epoxy resins

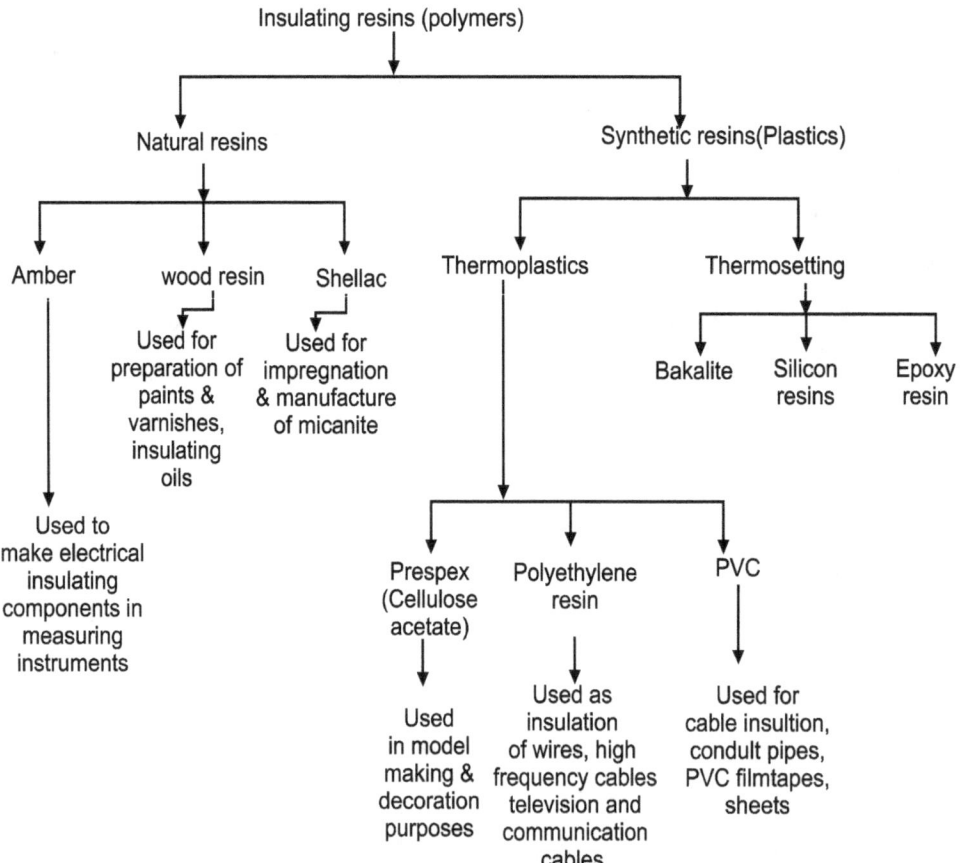

Fig. 2.3 : Classification of insulating resins

(i) Bakelite

- It is a type of phenol formaldehyde.
- It is hard, dark coloured thermosetting resins.
- Low softening temperature.
- Good electrical properties.
- Good mouldability, toughness.
- Good impact strength.

Applications

It is a widely used for manufacturing of lamp holders, switches, plug sockets and bases, and small panel boards.

(ii) Silicon Resins

- There are organic compounds of silicon.
- They are chemically inert and resistant to weather effects.
- They are heat resistant.
- Good water repellent.
- Its dielectric strength is 8 to 12 kV/mm.

Applications

- They are used as cooling and impregnating liquids for capacitors and transformers. They are also used to make silicon rubber when added with rubber.
- Used as mouldings for high temperature applications.
- Used as varnishes.

(iii) Epoxy Resins

- They are of transparent light amber colour.
- They have good mechanical strength, less shrinkage.
- It is good adhesive metal.
- As coating material, they shown superior toughness, elasticity and chemical resistance.

Applications

- It is used in manufacturing of laminated insulating boards.
- Used as insulating varnishes.
- Used as insulating material in cable end boxes, cable point boxes, instrument transformer etc.

2.4   LIQUID INSULATING MATERIALS

These are the organic liquids which are used as insulation, coolant and as dielectric.

2.4.1 Properties of Good Liquid Insulating Materials

- High flash point.
- Low viscosity.
- High or low dielectric constant (depending on application).
- Low dissipation factor (tan δ).
- Good arc quenching properties.
- They should have high dielectric strength.
- High thermal conductivity and specific heat.
- Resistivity should be high (more than 10^{16} Ωm).
- Non-inflammable and non-toxic.
- Low density.
- Low volatile.

Applications

It is used in

- Circuit breakers
- Capacitors
- Cables
- Transformer

Liquid insulating materials have the following types

2.4.2 Mineral Insulating Oil (Petroleum Oil or Transformer Oil)

- Most widely used liquid insulation in industry.
- Dissipation factor (tan δ) at 90°C is 0.001 to 0.005.
- Its resistivity at 90°C is 22000 Ωm.
- Permittivity is 2.1 to 2.5.
- Breakdown voltage is 30 to 50 kV/2.5 mm.
- These are obtained from crude petroleum by distillation of various by-products obtained.

Applications

- Low viscosity oil is used in high tension oil filled cables, transformer.
- Medium viscosity oil is used in switch gears and cables.
- High viscosity oil is used in gas filled cables and solid cables.
- Mostly used as insulation and as coolant in transformer.

2.4.3 Synthetic Liquids

- These are more expensive than mineral oil due to their high manufacturing cost.
- It is non-inflammable and non-explosive.
- Dissipation factor (tan δ) is less than 0.0005
- Permittivity is 2.1 to 2.2.
- It has high breakdown strength 40 to 60 kV/2.5 mm.
- Limitation of mineral oils such as easy oxidation, quick degradation of insulating and chemical properties, inflammable nature are overcome in this.
- E.g. Askarels, Arodors, Pyranols etc.

Applications

- Used in circuit breakers.
- Used in high pressure gas filled power cables and in D.C. capacitors.
- Used in high voltage transformer as coolant and insulation.

2.4.4 Askarel

- It is fire resistant.
- It has good insulating properties.
- It is costlier than transformer oil.
- Its resistivity is 10^{12} Ω-cm.
- Its permittivity is 4.8 to 5.3.
- Its breakdown voltage is 20 to 45 kV/2.5 mm.

Applications

- Used in circuit breakers.
- Used as a coolant for transformer and for capacitors operating at higher voltage.

2.4.5 Varnish

- When varnish is applied to a surface, it dries by either evaporation or by chemical action resulting in hard shining coating which is resistant to air and water.
- Varnishes protect the materials against moisture, dirt and dust.
- Varnishes are required in certain insulating system to
  - Give fire proof finish.
  - Protect from atmospheric corrosion and moisture.
  - Reduce degradation caused by oxidation.

- Improve insulation properties.
- Increase mechanical strength.
- The raw materials used for manufacture of varnishes are oils, solvents, thinners, resins and dryers.
- Different type of varnishes are

(a) Impregnating Varnishes

- These are used with porous and fibrous insulating materials like paper, fabrics, glass.
- Used in transformers, capacitors, motor winding etc.

(b) Coating Varnishes

- These are used when tough, smooth and glossy film is required to protect a substance from oxidation, corrosion, moisture absorption and solvent attract.
- These varnishes increases the mechanical strength of an assembly and surface leakage resistivity.

(c) Adhesive Varnishes

- They are used as binders for mica, glass and other insulating systems.

2.4.6 Enamel

- It is applied on conducting surface.
- They are also used to furnish a heavy protective coating on electronic equipment.
- It is a fusible insulated coating of organic base material.
- The maximum thickness of enamel coating is 0.05 mm.

Applications

- The enamel coating is provided on copper or aluminium wires which are used for winding in case of transformer motor etc.

2.5 GASES INSULATING MATERIALS

(a) Air

- It is naturally and abundantly available gaseous insulator.
- It needs no processing and can be used directly.
- Its dielectric strength is 30 kV/cm at 50 Hz.
- Its dielectric strength increases linearly with increase in gas pressure.

Applications

- It provides insulation between overhead transmission lines.
- Also used for cooling rotating parts of machine.
- Used in capacitors, as dielectric.
- Used in small transformers as coolant.

(b) Hydrogen (H_2)

- Very light gas.

- Thermal conductivity is 6.69 times of air.

- It has density 0.07 times that of air, so windage looses in machines can be minimised.

Applications

- Used as coolant in electric machine due to which efficiency increases.

- Used to reduce windage loss in high speed machines.

- Large turbo-generators and synchronous condensers are now-a-days hydrogen cooled.

(c) Nitrogen (N_2)

- Its density is 0.97 times that of air.

- Its thermal conductivity is 1.08 times that of air.

- In many high voltage applications air is replaced by nitrogen to prevent oxidation of the other insulating materials.

- Under pressure, it is used as the only insulator in certain capacitors.

- In high voltage gas pressure cables, pressurized nitrogen gas is used alongwith oil impregnated paper.

(d) Sulphur Hexafluoride (SF_6)

When sulphur is burnt is an atmosphere of fluorine, sulphur hexafluoride is formed.

It possess following properties

1. Physical Properties

- Colourless.

- Odourless.

- Non-toxic (pure SF_6 is non-toxic to health).

- Non-inflammable.

- Heat transfer ability is 2.5 times greater than air.

2. Chemical Properties

- It is stable upto 500°C.

- It is chemically inert so life of metallic parts, contacts is more.

- It is electro-negative gas.

- It has electron affinity so arc quenches quickly. Thus, it has excellent arc quenching properties.

3. Dielectric Properties

- Dielectric strength of SF_6 gas at atmosphere pressure is 2.35 times that of air but less than oil by 30%.

- But when pressure of SF_6 gas is more than 3 kg/cm², its dielectric strength is higher than oil.

Applications of SF_6 Gas

- It is widely used in electrical equipments like high voltage switch gears, capacitors, cables, circuit breakers.

- The most important application is Gas Insulated Substation (GIS).

SOLVED EXAMPLES

Example 2.1 : The resistivity of the insulation material in a cable having conductor diameter of 1.8 cm and sheath diameter of 5 cm. If the length of cable is 3000 m and its insulation resistance is 1820 MΩ.

Solution : Given,

$$d_1 = 1.8 \text{ cm}$$
$$d_2 = 5 \text{ cm}$$
$$\therefore \quad R_1 = 1.8/2 = 0.9 \text{ cm}$$
$$R_2 = 5/2 = 2.5 \text{ cm}$$

We know that R_i = Insulation resistance

$$= \frac{\rho_i}{2\pi l} \log_e \left(\frac{R_2}{R_1}\right)$$

$$1820 \times 10^6 = \frac{\rho_i}{2\pi \times 3000} \log_e \left(\frac{2.5}{0.9}\right)$$

$$\rho_i = 33.1 \times 10^{12} \ \Omega m$$

Example 2.2 : A parallel plate capacitor is to be made to store 20 μC at a potential of 10 kV. The separation between the plates is 5×10^{-4} m. If the dielectric constant of material is 10 kept between plates, the area that the plates must have is?

Solution : Given,

$$Q = 20 \ \mu C$$
$$V = 10 \text{ kV}$$
$$d = 5 \times 10^{-4}$$
$$\varepsilon_r = 10$$

$$C = \frac{Q}{V}$$

$$= \frac{20 \times 10^{-6}}{10 \times 10^3}$$

$$\boxed{C = 2 \times 10^{-9} \text{ F}}$$

We know that, $\qquad\qquad C = \dfrac{\varepsilon_0 \, \varepsilon_r \, A}{d}$

$$A = \dfrac{C_d}{\varepsilon_0 \, \varepsilon_r}$$

$$A = \dfrac{2 \times 10^{-9} \times 5 \times 10^{-4}}{8.85 \times 10^{-12} \times 10}$$

$$\boxed{A = 10.294 \times 10^{-3} \text{ m}}$$

Example 2.3 : What will be insulation resistance of single core cable having inside diameter 0.03 m outside diameter 0.075 m length 2 km and the resistivity of insulating material 6×10^{12} Ωm.

Solution : Given, $\qquad\qquad d_1 = 0.03$

$$d_2 = 0.075$$

$$l = 2 \text{ km}$$

$$\rho_i = 6 \times 10^{12} \ \Omega \text{ m}$$

We know that, $\qquad\qquad R_i = \dfrac{\rho_i}{2\pi\lambda} \log_e \left(\dfrac{R_2}{R_1}\right)$

$$R_2 = \dfrac{d_2}{2} = \dfrac{0.075}{2} = 0.0375 \text{ m}$$

$$R_1 = \dfrac{d_1}{2} = \dfrac{0.03}{2} = 0.015 \text{ m}$$

$$R_i = \dfrac{6 \times 10^{12}}{2\pi \times 2000} \log_e \left(\dfrac{0.0375}{0.015}\right)$$

$$= \dfrac{3 \times 10^9}{2\pi} \log_e \left(\dfrac{0.0375}{0.015}\right)$$

$$R_i = 4.37 \times 10^8 \ \Omega$$

Example 2.4 : Resistance of conductor for 6.5 km long cable has conductor diameter of 15 mm if specific resistance of conductor material is 0.017 micro Ωm.

Solution : Given, $\qquad\qquad l = 6.5 \text{ km}$

$$r = 15 \text{ mm}$$

$$\rho = 0.017 \ \mu \Omega \text{ m}$$

$$\text{Area} = \pi r^2 = \pi \left(\dfrac{15 \times 10^{-2}}{2}\right)^2$$

$$= 0.01767$$

$$R_c = \dfrac{\rho l}{\text{Area}} = \dfrac{0.017 \times 10^{-6} \times 6500}{0.01767}$$

$$\boxed{R_c = 0.3126 \ \Omega}$$

QUESTIONS

1. Explain properties of a good insulating materials.
2. Classify insulating materials on the basis of limiting temperature. Give two examples in each class.
3. State the properties and applications of
   (a)   Asbestos   (b)   Ceramics
   (c)   Porcelain   (d)   Mica
4. Classify gaseous insulating materials. Give examples in each case.
5. Write short note on 'Impregnation process'.
6. List insulating materials used for
   (a) power cables   (b)   line insulators
7. Write a short note on 'Crystal defects'.
8. List insulating materials use for power cable and line insulators.
9. Write short note on
   (i)   Mica   (ii) Asbestos
   (iii) Press board   (iv) Porcelain
   (v) SF_6
10. Short note on liquid insulating materials.
11. What is thermal classification of insulating materials?
12. What is impregnation process? Why it is necessary? Explain impregnation process for paper and cotton.
13. Sate properties and applications of
    (a) SF_6 (b)   Transformer oil
    (c) Micanite   (d)   Ceramics
14. Discuss insulating materials used for
    (a) Rotating machines   (b)   Capacitors
15. Discuss insulating materials used for
    (a) Power transformer   (b)   Switch gears
16. Discuss insulating materials used for
    (a) Power transformer   (b)   Switch gears
17. Give properties and application of
    (a) Askarel   (b) SF_6
    (c) Pressboard   (d)   Mica

18. What are ceramics? Give their properties and applications? What is effect of temperature and moisture on ceramics?

19. State the properties and applications of

    (a) Transformer oil   (b) SF_6

20. What is impregnation process? Why it is necessary? Explain impregnation process for paper and cotton.

21. Discuss insulating materials used for power capacitors and cables.

22. Discuss insulating materials used for

    (a) Power transformer   (b)   Line insulators

23. State the properties and applications of

    (a) Transformer oil   (b) SF_6

24. What do you mean by fibrous insulating material? What is their major drawback? How it can be overcome?

25. Discuss insulating materials used for power and distribution transformer.

26. Discuss the insulating materials used for

    (a) Power transformer   (b)   Power cables

27. State the properties and application of

    (a) SF_6 gas   (b)   Transformer oil

    (c) Micanate   (d)   Ceramics

28. Write down properties and applications of

    (a) Paper   (b)   Press board

    (c) Fibrous materials   (d)   Ceramics

    (e) Asbestos   (f)   Varnish

    (g) Askarel   (h)   Insulating gases like air

    (i) SF_6 gas

29. Describe the insulating materials used in

    (a) Switch gears   (b)   Line insulators

30. State the properties and applications of

    (i) Porcelain   (ii) SF_6 gas

31. Discuss the insulating materials used for power transformers.

32. What is impregnation process? Why is it necessary for fibrous insulating materials? Explain impregnation process for paper and cotton.

33. Discuss the insulating materials used for

   (i) Power transformer   (ii)   Line insulators

34. State the properties and applications of

   (i) SF$_6$ gas   (ii)   Ceramics

   (iii) Asbestos   (iv)   Transformer oil

35. State the properties and applications of

   (i) Mica   (ii)   Transformer oil

36. Discuss insulating materials used for

   (i) Capacitors   (ii)   Switchgears

37. Write down properties and applications of the following

   (i) Paper and press board (ii)   SF$_6$ gas

   (iii) Ceramics   (iv)   Mica and asbestos

✠ ✠ ✠

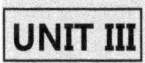

MAGNETIC MATERIALS

3.1 INTRODUCTION

A magnetic field consists of imaginary lines of flux coming from moving or spinning electrically charged particles. What a magnetic field actually consists of is somewhat of a mystery, but we do know it is a special property of space.

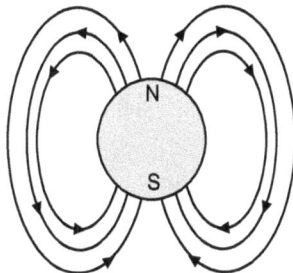

Fig. 3.1 : Magnetic field or lines of flux of a moving charged particle

Names of Poles

The lines of magnetic flux flow from one end of the object to the other. By convention, we call one end of a magnetic object the North-seeking pole and the other the South-seeking pole, as refferd to the Earth's North and South magnetic poles. The magnetic flux is defined as moving from N to S.

Magnets

Although individual particles such as electrons can have magnetic fields, larger objects such as a piece of iron also have a magnetic field. If a larger object exhibits a sufficiently great magnetic field, it is called a magnet.

3.2 MAGNETIC STORE

The magnetic field of an object can create a magnetic force on other objects with magnetic fields. That force is call magnetism.

When a magnetic field is applied to a moving electric charge, such as a moving proton or the electrical current in a wire, the force on the charge is called a Lorentz force.

Attraction

When two magnets or magnetic objects are close to each other, there is a force that attracts the poles together.

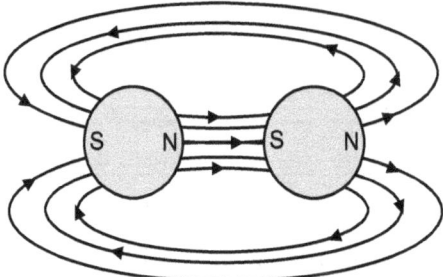

Fig. 3.2 : Force attracts N to S

Magnets also strongly attract ferromagnetic materials such as iron, nickel and cobalt.

Repulsion

When two magnetic objects have like poles facing each other, the magnetic force pushes them apart.

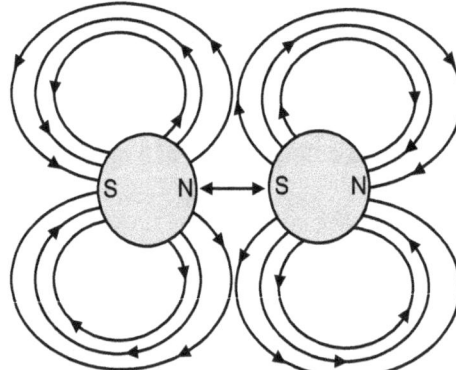

Fig. 3.3 : Force pushes magnetic objects apart

Magnets can also weakly repel diamagnetic materials.

3.3   MAGNETIC AND ELECTRIC FIELDS

Electric Charges and Magnetism Similar

Just as the positive and negative electrical charges attract each other, the N and S poles of a magnet attract each other.

In electricity like charges repel, and in magnetism like poles repel.

Electric Charges and Magnetism Different

The magnetic field is a dipole field. That means that every magnet must have two poles.

On the other hand, a positive (+) or negative (−) electrical charge can stand alone. Electrical charges are thus called monopoles, since they can exist without the opposite charge. Define magnetic susceptibility magnetic moment.

3.4   MAGNETIC SUSCEPTIBILITY

Magnetic susceptibility is the degree to which a material can be magnetized in an external magnetic field. If the ratio between the induced magnetization and the inducing field is expressed per unit volume this volume susceptibility (k) is defined as

$$k = M/H,$$

where M is the volume magnetization induced in a material of susceptibility k by the applied external field H. Volume susceptibility is a dimensionless quantity.

3.4.1 Magnetic Moments

Magnetic moments are permanent dipole moments within the atom which are made up from electrons angular momentum and spin.

Electrons inside atoms contribute magnetic moments from their angular momentum and from their orbital momentum around the nucleus. Magnetic moments from the nucleus are insignificant in contrast to magnetic moments from electrons. Thermal contribution in this will result in higher energy electrons causing disruption to their order and alignment between dipoles to be destroyed.

3.5   TYPES OF MAGNETISM

All magnetic materials contain magnetic moments, which behave in a way similar to microscopic bar magnetis These are principally: paramagnets, ferromagnets, antiferromagnets and ferrimagnets.

Paramagnetism

In a paramagnet, the magnetic moments tend to be randomly orientated due to thermal fluctuations when there is no magnetic field. In an applied magnetic field these moments start to align parallel to the field such that the magnetisation of the material is proportional to the applied field.

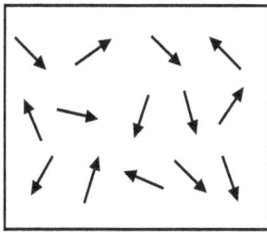

Fig. 3.4 (a) : Schematic showing the magnetic dipole moments randomly aligned in a paramagnetic sample

Ferromagnetism

The magnetic moments in a ferromagnet have the tendency to aligned parallel to each other under the influence of a magnetic field. though, unlike the moments in a paramagnet, these moments will then remain parallel when a magnetic field is not applied.

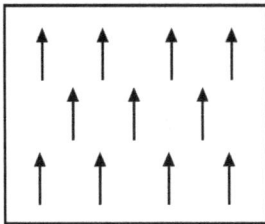

Fig. 3.4 (b) : Schematic showing the magnetic dipole moments aligned parallel in a ferromagnetic material

Antiferromagnetism

Adjacent magnetic moments from the magnetic ions tend to align anti-parallel to each other without an applied field. In case, adjacent magnetic moments are equal in magnitude and opposite therefore there is no overall magnetisation.

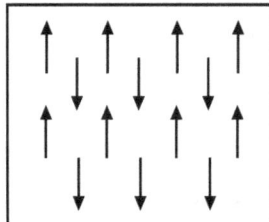

Fig. 3.4 (c) : Schematic showing adjacent magnetic dipole moments with equal magnitude aligned anti-parallel in an antiferromagnetic material. This is only one of many possible antiferromagnetic arrangements of magnetic moments.

Ferrimagnetism

The aligned magnetic moments are not of the identical size; that is more than one type of magnetic ion. An overall magnetisation is produced but not all the magnetic moments may give a positive contribution to the overall magnetisation.

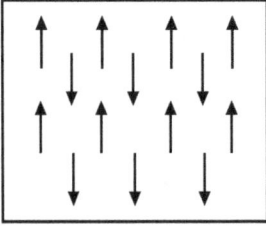

Fig. 3.4 (d) : Schematic showing adjacent magnetic moments of different magnitudes aligned anti-parallel.

Below is a periodic table showing the elements and the types of magnetism at room temperature:

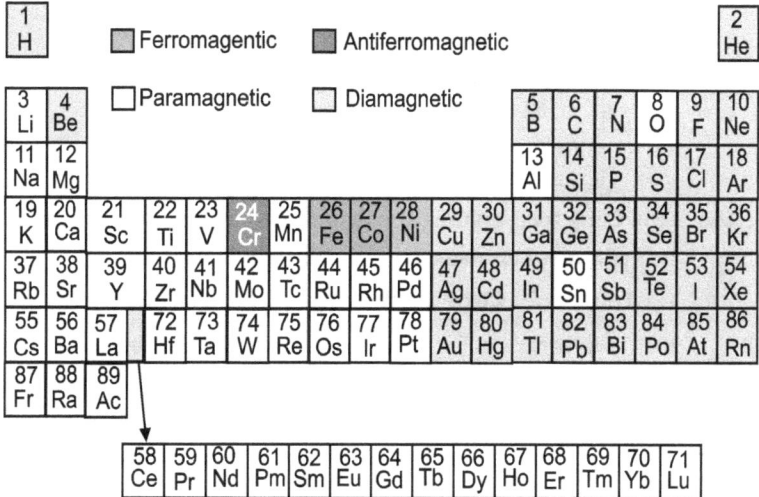

Fig. 3.4 (e) : Diagram of a periodic table showing elements coloured according to the type of magnetism they show at room temperature.

3.6 CURIE TEMPERATURE

In physics and materials science, the Curie temperature (T_c), or Curie point, is the temperature where a material's permanent magnetism changes to induced magnetism. The force of magnetism is determined by magnetic moments.

The Curie Temperature is the critical point where a material's intrinsic magnetic moments change direction. Magnetic moments in material are permanent dipole moments within the atom which originate from electrons angular momentum and spin. At a material's Curie Temperature those intrinsic magnetic moments change direction.

Permanent magnetism is caused by the alignment of magnetic moments and induced magnetism is created when disordered magnetic moments are forced to align in an applied magnetic field. For example, the ordered magentic moments ferromagnetic, Fig. 3.5 change and become disordered paramagnetic Fig. 3.6 at the Curie Temperature.

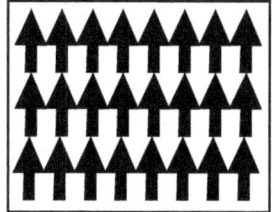

Fig. 3.5. : Below the Curie temperature, neighbouring magnetic spins align in a ferromagnet in the absence of an applied magnetic field

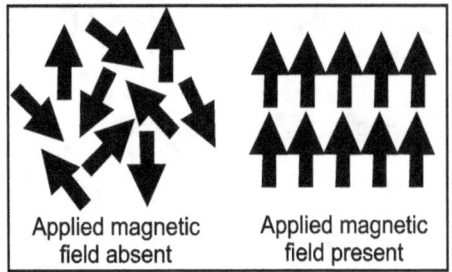

Applied magnetic field absent   Applied magnetic field present

Fig. 3.6 : Above the Curie temperature, the magnetic spins are randomly aligned in a paramagnet unless a magnetic field is applied

Table 3.1 : Curie Temperature of Materials

Material	Curie Temperature (K)
Iron (Fe)	1043
Cobalt (Co)	1400
Nickel (Ni)	631
Gadolinium (Gd)	292
Dysprosium (Dy)	88
MnBi	630
CrO_2	386
MnAs	318
EuO	69
Iron (III) Oxide (Fe_2O_3)	948
Iron (II, III) oxide (FeO Fe_2O_3)	858
$NiOFe_2O_3$	858
$CuOFe_2O_3$	728
$MgOFe_2O_3$	713
$MnOFe_2O_3$	573
$Y_3Fe_5O_{12}$	560

Higher temperatures compose magnets weaker as spontaneous magnetism only occurs below the Curie Temperature. Magnetic susceptibility only occurs above the Curie Temperature and can be calculated from the Curie-Weiss Law which is derived from Curie's Law.

In analogy to ferromagnetic and paramagnetic materials, the Curie temperature can also describe the temperature where a material's spontaneous electric polarisation changes to induced electric polarisation or the reverse upon reduction of the temperature below the Curie temperature.

The Curie temperature is named after Pierre Curie who showed that magnetism was lost at a critical temperature.

3.6.1 Curie-Weiss Law

The Curie-Weiss law is model derived from a mean-field approximation, this means it works well for the materials temperature,T, much greater than their corresponding Curie Temperature,T_c, i.e. T >> T_c; however fails to describe the magnetic susceptibility, χBoth Curie's law and the Curie-Weiss law do not hold for T < T_c.

Curie's law for a paramagnetic material;

$$\chi = \frac{M}{H} = \frac{M \, m_0}{B} = \frac{C}{T}$$

where,

  χ : The magnetic susceptibility; the influence of an applied magnetic field on a material.

  M: The magnetic moments per unit volume.

  H : The macroscopic magnetic field.

  B : The magnetic field.

  C : The material-specific curie constant.

$$C = \frac{m_0 \, m_B^2}{3k_B} \, Ng^2 \, J \, (J + 1)$$

where,

  m_0 : The permeability of free space. In CGS units is taken to equal one.

  g   : The Lande g-factor.

  J (J + 1): The eigenvalue for eigenstate J^2 for the stationary states within the incomplete atoms shells (electrons unpaired.

  m_B : the Bohr Magneton

  k_B : Boltzmann's constant

Total Magnetism : is N number of magnetic moments per unit volume.

The Curie-Weiss law is then derived from Curie's law to be

$$\chi = \frac{C}{T - T_c}$$

where, $T_C = \frac{C\lambda}{mo}$

λ is the Weiss molecular field constant.

Materials with magnetic moments that change properties at the Curie temperature

Ferromagnetic, paramagnetic, ferrimagnetic and antiferromagnetic structures are made up of intrinsic magnetic moments. If all electrons within the structure are paired, these moments cancel out due to having opposite spins and angular momentum with in them. Thus even with an applied magnetic field will have different properties and no Curie Temperature.

Below T_c	Above T_c
Ferromagnetic	↔ Paramagnetic
Ferrimagnetic	↔ Paramagnetic
Antiferromagnetic	↔ Paramagnetic

3.6.2 Physics of Curie Temperature

As the Curie-Weiss Law is an approximation a more accurate model is needed when the temperature, approaches the materials Curie Temperature, T_C.

Magnetic susceptibility occurs above the Curie Temperature.

An accurate model of critical behaviour for magnetic susceptibility with critical exponent γ;

$$X \sim \frac{1}{(T - T_c)^\gamma}$$

The critical exponent differs between materials and for the mean-field model is taken as γ=1.

As temperature is inversely proportional to magnetic susceptibility when T approaches T_C the denominator tends to zero and the magnetic susceptibility approaches infinity allowing magnetism to occur. This is a spontaneous magnetism which is a property of ferromagnetic and ferrimagnetic materials.

Approaching Curie Temperature from Below

Magnetism depends on temperature and spontaneous magnetism occurs below the Curie Temperature. An accurate model of critical behaviour for spontaneous magnetism with critical exponent β;

$$M \sim (T - T_c)^\beta$$

The critical exponent differs between materials and for the mean-field model as taken as β = 0.5 where T << T_C.

The spontaneous magnetism approaches zero as the temperature increases towards the materials Curie Temperature.

Approaching Absolute Zero (0 Kelvin)

The spontaneous magnetism, occurring in ferromagnetic, ferrimagnetic and antiferromagnetic materials, approaches zero as the temperature increases towards the Curie Temperature. Spontaneous magnetism is at its maximum as the temperature approaches 0. the magnetic moments are completely aligned and at their strongest magnitude of magnetism due to no thermal disturbance.

In paramagnetic materials temperature is sufficient to overcome the ordered alignments. As the temperature approaches 0 K the entropy decreases to zero.Both Curie's Law and the Curie-Weiss law fail as the temperature approaches 0 K. This is because they depend on the magnetic susceptibility which only applies when the state is disordered.

Gadolinium Sulphate continues to satisfy Curie's law at 1 K. Between 0-1 K the law fails to hold and a sudden change in the intrinsic structure occurs at the Curie Temperature.

Weiss Domains and Surface and Bulk Curie Temperatures

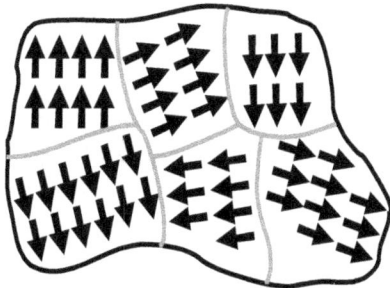

Fig. 3.7 : The Weiss domains in a ferromagnetic material; the magnetic moments are aligned in domains

Materials structures consist of intrinsic magnetic moments which are separated into domains called Weiss domains. This can result in ferromagnetic materials having no spontaneous magnetism as domains. The position of particles can therefore have different orientations around the surface than the main part of the material. This property directly affects the Curie Temperature as there can be a bulk Curie Temperature T_B and a different surface Curie Temperature T_S for a material.

This allows for the surface Curie Temperature to be ferromagnetic above the bulk Curie Temperature when the main state is disordered, i.e. Ordered and disordered states occur simultaneously.

3.6.3 Factors affecting on Curie Temperature

- **Composite Materials**

Composite materials, other materials with different properties, can change the Curie Temperature. For example, a composite which has silver it can create spaces for oxygen molecules in bonding which decreases the Curie Temperature as the crystal lattice will not be as compact.

The alignment of magnetic moments in the composite material affects the Curie Temperature. If the materials moments are parallel with each other the Curie Temperature will increase and if perpendicular the Curie Temperature will decreaseas either more or less thermal energy will be needed to destroy the alignments.

- **Particle Size**

The size of particles in a material's crystal lattice changes the Curie Temperature. Due to the small size of particles the fluctuations of electron spins become more prominent, this results in the Curie Temperature drastically decreasing when the size of particles decrease as the fluctuations cause disorder. The size of a particle also affects the anisotropy causing alignment to become less stable and thus lead to confusion in magnetic moments.

The extreme of this is super magnetism which only occurs in small ferromagnetic particles and is where fluctuations are very influential causing magnetic moments to change direction randomly and thus create disorder.

- **Pressure**

Pressure changes a material's Curie Temperature. Pressure directly affects the kinetic energy in particles as movement increases causing the vibrations to disrupt the order of magnetic moments. This is similar to temperature as it also increases the kinetic energy of particles and destroys the order of magnetic moments and magnetism.

- **Orbital Ordering**

Orbital ordering changes the Curie Temperature of a material. Orbital ordering can be controlled through applied strains. This is a function that determines the wave of a single electron or paired electrons inside the material. Having control over the probability of where the electron will be allows the Curie Temperature to be altered. For example, the delocalised electrons can be moved onto the same plane by applied strains within the crystal lattice.

The Curie Temperature is seen to increase greatly due to electrons being packed together in the same plane, they are forced to align due to the exchange interaction and thus increases the strength of the magnetic moments which prevents thermal disorder at lower temperatures.

3.6.4 Curie Temperature in Ferroelectric and Piezoelectric Materials

In analogy to ferromagnetic and paramagnetic materials, the Curie Temperature can also used to describe the temperature where a material's spontaneous electric polarisation changes to induced electric polarisation, or vice versa.

Electric polarisation is a result of aligned electric dipoles. Aligned electric dipoles are composites of positive and negative charges The charges are separated from their stable placement in the particles and can occur spontaneously, from pressure or an applied electric field.

Ferroelectric, dielectric (paraelectric) and piezoelectric materials have electric polarisation. In ferroelectric materials, there is a spontaneous electric polarisation in the absence of an applied electric field. In dielectric materials, there is electric polarisation aligned only when an electric field is applied. Piezoelectric materials have electric polarisation due to applied mechanical stress distorting the structure from pressure.

T_0 is the temperature where ferroelectric materials lose their spontaneous polarisation as a first or second order phase change occurs, that is the internal structure changes or the internal symmetry changes. In certain cases, T_0 is equal to the Curie Temperature.

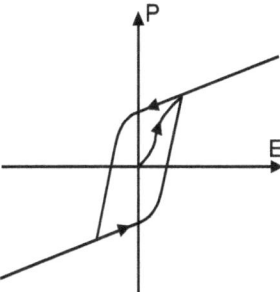

Fig. 3.8 : Ferroelectric polarisation P in an applied electric field E.

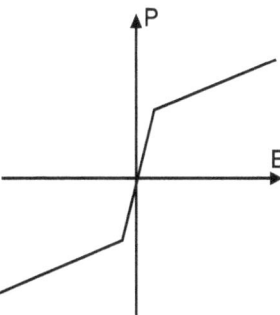

Fig. 3.9 : Dielectric polarisation P in an applied electric field E.

Below T_0	Above T_0
Ferroelectric	↔ Dielectric

3.7 CLASSIFICATION OF MAGNETIC MATERIALS

3.7.1 Paramagnetic

A material is paramagnetic only above its Curie Temperature. Paramagnetic materials are non-magnetic when a magnetic field is absent and magnetic when a magnetic field is applied. When the magnetic field is missing the material has disordered magnetic moments; that is, the atoms are unsymmetrical and not aligned. When the magnetic field is present the magnetic moments are provisionally realigned parallel to the applied field; the atoms are symmetrical and aligned. The magnetic moment in the same direction is what causes an induced magnetic field.

For paramagnetism The magnetic susceptibility only applies above the Curie Temperature for disordered states.

Sources of Paramagnetism (Materials which have Curie Temperatures)

- All atoms which have unpaired electrons.
- Atoms where inner shells are incomplete in electrons.
- Free radicals.
- Metals

Above the Curie Temperature the atoms are excited, the spin orientation becomes randomised but can be realigned in an applied field and the material paramagnetic. Below the Curie Temperature the intrinsic structure gone a phase transition, the atoms are ordered and the material is ferromagnetic. The paramagnetic materials induced magnetic fields are very weak in comparison to ferromagnetic materials magnetic fields.

3.7.2 Ferromagnetic

Materials are only ferromagnetic below their corresponding Curie temperatures. Ferromagnetic materials are magnetic in the absence of an applied magnetic field.

The magnetic interactions are held together by exchange interactions; otherwise thermal disorder would overcome the weak interactions of magnetic moments. The exchange interaction has a zero probability of parallel electrons occupying the same point in time, implying a preferred parallel alignment in the material. The Boltzmann factor contributes heavily prefers interacting particles to be aligned in the same direction. This causes ferromagnets to have strong magnetic fields and high Curie temperatures .

Below the Curie temperature, the atoms are aligned and parallel, causing spontaneous magnetism; the material is ferromagnetic. Above the Curie temperature the material is paramagnetic, as the atoms lose their ordered magnetic moments when the material undergoes a phase transition.

3.7.3 Ferrimagnetic

Materials are only ferrimagnetic below their materials corresponding Curie Temperature. Ferrimagnetic materials are magnetic in the absence of an applied magnetic field and are made up of two different ions.

When a magnetic field is absent the material has a spontaneous magnetism which is of ordered magnetic moments; that is, for ferrimagnetism one ion's magnetic moments are aligned facing in one direction with certain magnitude and the other ion's magnetic moments are aligned facing in the opposite direction with a different magnitude. As result there is still a spontaneous magnetism and a magnetic field is present.

3.7.4 Antiferromagnetic and the Néel Temperature

Antiferromagnetic materials are weakly magnetic in the absence or presence of an applied magnetic field. Materials are only antiferromagetic below their corresponding Néel Temperature. This is similar to the Curie Temperature as above the Néel Temperature the material undergoes a phase transition and becomes paramagnetic.

The material has equal magnetic moments aligned in opposite directions resulting in a zero magnetic moment and a net magnetism of zero at all temperatures below the Neel Temperature. Antiferromagnetic materials are weakly magnetic in the absence or presence of an applied magnetic field.

Similar to ferromagnetic materials the magnetic interactions are held together by exchange interactions preventing thermal disorder from overcoming the weak interactions of magnetic moments.

3.7.5 Piezoelectric

An external force applies pressure on particles inside the material which affects the structure of the crystal lattice. Particles become unsymmetrical which allows a net polarisation from each particle. Symmetry would cancel the opposing charges out and there would be no net polarisation. Below the transition temperature T_0 displacement of electric charges causes polarisation. Above the transition temperature T_0 the structure is cubic and symmetric, causing the material to become dielectric. Electric charges are also agitated and disordered causing the material to have no electric polarisation in the absence of an applied electric field.

Ferroelectric and Dielectric

Materials are only ferroelectric below their corresponding transition temperature T_0. Ferroelectric materials are all piezoelectric and therefore have a spontaneous electric polarisation as the structures are unsymmetrical.

Materials are only dielectric above their corresponding transition temperature T_0. Dielectric materials have no electric polarisation in the absence of an applied electric field. The electric dipoles are unaligned and have no net polarisation. In analogy to magnetic susceptibility, electric susceptibility only occurs above T_0.

Ferroelectric materials when polarised are influenced under hysterisis Fig. 3.8 that is they are dependent on their past state as well as their current state. As an electric field is applied the dipoles are forced to align and polarisation is created, when the electric field is removed polarisation remains. The hysteresis loop depends on temperature and as a result as the temperature is increased and reaches T_0 the two curves become one curve as shown in the dielectric polarisation Fig. 3.9.

Relative Permittivity

A modified version of the Curie Weiss law applies to the dielectric constant, also known as the relative permittivity:

$$\varepsilon \ = \varepsilon_0 + \frac{C}{T - T_c}$$

3.8   TYPES OF MAGNETIC MATERIAL

Most of magnetic materials of industrial interests are ferromagenetic materials. The ferromagnetic materials can be categorized into two; one is soft magnetic materials and the other is hard magnetic materials. As shown in the magnetization curve, ferromagnetic materials with the demagnetized state does not show magnetization even though they have spontaneous magnetization. This is because the ferromagnetic materials are divided into many magnetic domains. Within the magnetic domains, the direction of magnetic moment is aligened. though, the direction of magnetic moments vary at magnetic domain walls so that it can reduce the magnetostatic energy in the total volume. In the demagnetized state, total magnetization is cancelled because of the random orientation of the magnetizations in magnetic domains. When external magnetic field is applied, domain walls migrate and disappear when all magnetic moments are aligened to the direction of the magnetic field. When all magnetic domains are wiped away and magnetizations are all aligned to the direction of the magnetic field, magnetization is saturated. This magnetization is called saturation magnetization M_s.

When domain wall can easily migrate, the ferromagnetic material can be easily magnetized at low magnetic filed. This type of ferromagnetic materials are called soft magnetic material. Since soft magnetic materials can be demagnetized at low magnetic field, coercivity H_c is low. As they can be easily magnetized, permeability is high. For ferromagnetic materials to be soft, their magnetocrystalline anisotropy and magnetostriction constant must be low. In addition, for easy migration of magnetic domains, they must have small number of defects such as crystal grains.

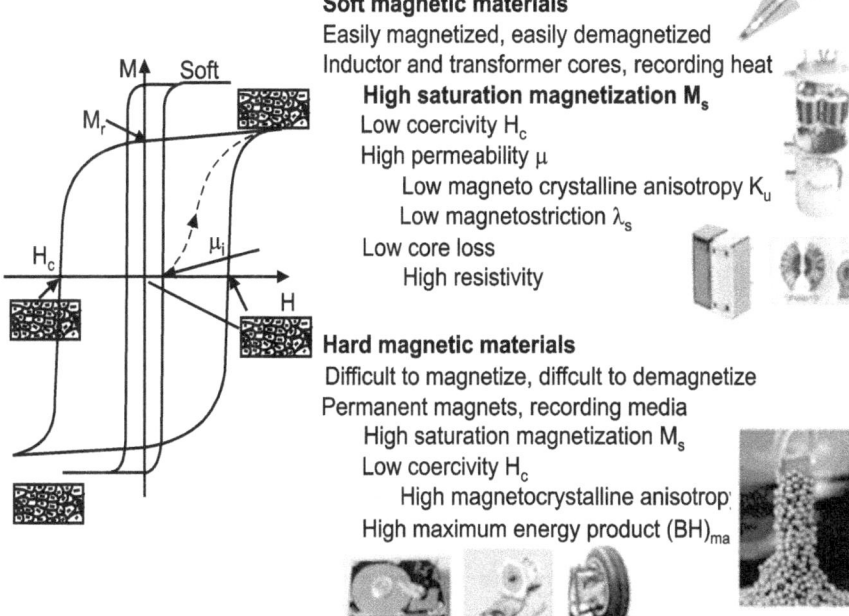

Soft magnetic materials
Easily magnetized, easily demagnetized
Inductor and transformer cores, recording heat
  High saturation magnetization M_s
  Low coercivity H_c
  High permeability μ
    Low magneto crystalline anisotropy K_u
    Low magnetostriction λ_s
  Low core loss
    High resistivity

Hard magnetic materials
 Difficult to magnetize, diffcult to demagnetize
Permanent magnets, recording media
  High saturation magnetization M_s
  Low coercivity H_c
    High magnetocrystalline anisotrop
  High maximum energy product $(BH)_{ma}$

Fig. 3.10

When domain wall is difficult to migrate, magnetization of the ferromagnetic material occurs only when large magnetic field is applied. In other words, this type of ferromagnetic materials are difficult ot magnetize, but once magnetized, it is difficult to demagnetize. These materials are called hard magnetic materials, and are suitable for applications such as permanent magnets and magnetic recording media. Hard magnetic materials have high magnetocrystalline anisotropy. Since large magnetic field is required to demagnetize, their coercivity H_c is usually high, but coercivity is highly sensitive to the microstructururure.

3.8.1 Differences between Hard and Soft Magnetic Materials

Sr. No.	Hard Magnetic Materials	Soft Magnetic Materials
1	Materials which retain their magnetism and are difficult to demagnetize are called hard magnetic materials. These materials retain their magnetism even after the removal of the applied magnetic field. Hence these materials are used for making permanent magnets. In permanent magnets the movement of the domain wall is prevented. They are	Soft magnetic materials are easy to magnetize and demagnetize. These materials are used for making temporary magnets. The domain wall movement is easy. Hence they are easy to magnetize. By annealing the cold worked material, the dislocation density is reduced and the domain wall movement is easier. Soft magnetic materials should not possess any void and its structure should be

	prepared by heating the magnetic materials to the required temperature and then quenching them. Impurities increase the strength of hard magnetic materials.	homogeneous so that the materials are not affected by impurities.
2	They have large hysteresis loss due to large hysteresis loop area.	They have low hysteresis loss due to small hysteresis area.
3	Susceptibility and permeability are low.	Susceptibility and permeability are high.
4	Coercivity and retentivity values are large.	Coercivity and retentivity values are less.
5	Magnetic energy stored is high.	Since they have low retentivity and coercivity, they are not used for making permanent magnets.
6	They possess high value of BH product.	Magnetic energy stored is less.
7	The eddy current loss is high.	The eddy current loss is less because of high resistivity.

Table 3.2 : Applications of Magnetic Materials

Field of application	Products	Requirements	Materials
Soft Magnets			
Power Conversation Electrical Mecahnical	Motors generators electromagnets	Large M_R Small H_C Low losses = small conductivity low ω	Fe based materials, e.g. Fe + $\approx$ (0.7 – 5)% Si Fe + $\approx$ (35 – 50)% Co
Power adaption	(Power) Transformers Transformer	Linear M – H curve	
Signal transfer	LF ("low" frequency; up to $\approx$ 100 kHz)	Small conductivity medium ω	Fe + $\approx$ 36% Fe/Ni/Co
	HF ("high" frequency up to $\approx$ 100 kHz)	Very small conductivity high ω	$\approx$ Ni-Zn ferrites
Magnetic field screening	"Mu-metal"	Large dM/dH for H $\approx$ 0 ideally	Ni/Fe/Cu/Cr$\approx$ 77/16/5/2
Hard Magnets			
Permanent magnets	small Loudspeaker	Large H_c (and M_R)	Fe/Co/Ni/Al/Cu $\approx$50/24/14/9/3

	small generators motoers sensors		$SmCo_5$ Sm_2CO_{17} "NdFeB" ($Nd_2Fe_{14}B$)
Data storage analog	Video tape audito tape Ferrite core memory drum	Medium H_c (and M_R) hystereses loop as rectangular as possible	NiCo CuNiFe CrO_2 Fe_2O_3
	Bubble memory	Special domain structure	Magentic garnets or $Gd_3 Ga_5O_{12}$
Specialities			
Quantum devises	GMR reading head MRAM	Special spin structures in multilayered materials	

3.9 APPLICATIONS OF FERROMAGNETIC MATERIALS

Magnetic Recording Materials

Magnetic materials like CrO_2 or Fe_2O_3 are use for recording. In this one is recording head which is consists of toroidals core made up of soft ferrite with coil and having air gap of 5 to 15 mm as shown in Fig. 3.11 This air gap responds to electrical signal and creates magnetic pattern on tape.

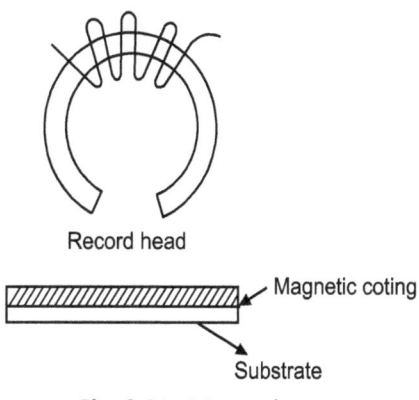

Record head

Magnetic coting

Substrate

Fig. 3.11 : Magnetic tape

Compact Disc

Compact disc also known as CD which is optical disc used to store digital data. In this, data is stored as a series of tiny indentations known as pits area between pits known as lands. Different types of CDs are :

- Video CD (VCD)
- Super Audio CD
- Recordable CD
- Recordable Audio CD
- Re-writable CD (CD-RW)

3.9.1 Introduction to Laser and Magnetic Strip

Laser is stands for light amplification by stimulated emission of radiation. Laser light is concentrated and travels as tight unbroken beam. This light does not disperse as it moves from origin of it. Laser light is monochromatic having single wavelength which corresponds to one specific colour.

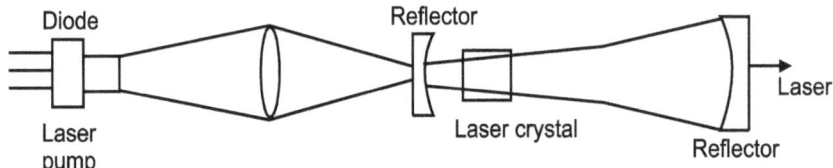

Fig. 3.12

Applications

- Bore holes in the harder substance like diamond.
- Use for delicate surgeries.
- Use at NASA for remote sensing.
- Use as cutting tool for other substance.

Magnetic Strip Technology

- This is a technology carries data stored within a thin strip of magnetic media.
- Strip is adhered to the paper or plastic card.
- It is swiped through a magnetic reader to get back data stored in it.
- It has two tracks. Track 1 has 79 characters and Track 2 has 40 characters at the maximum.

Applications

- Swap card.
- ATM card.
- Card key's of hotels.

SOLVED EXAMPLES

Example 3.1 : Determine the percentage change in hysteresis and eddy current of a ferromagnetic material loss if supply frequency is increased by 10% the supply voltage and size of the specimen remaining unchanged.

Solution : Hysteresis loss at frequency f

$$W_h = A \cdot f$$

When f is increased by 10%

$$W_h = A(f + 0.1f) = 1.1 \, A \cdot f$$

Change in W_h $= 0.1 \, A \cdot f$

$\therefore$ % change in W_h = $\dfrac{0.1 \, A \cdot f \times 100}{A \cdot f} = 10\%$

Eddy current loss at frequency f,

$$W_e = B \cdot f^2$$

When f is increased by 10%

$$W'_e = B \cdot (1.1 \, f)^2$$
$$= 1.21 \, B \cdot f^2$$

$\therefore$ % change in We = $\dfrac{1.21 \, Bf^2 - Bf^2}{Bf^2} = 21\%$

Example 3.2 : Calculate hysteresis loss in a specimen of iron subjected to a magnetization of 60 Hz. The weight of the specimen is 40 kg and its density is 8000 kg/m^3. Hysteresis loop area is equivalent to 200 J/m^3. What will be hysteresis loss of the specimen at 50 Hz.

Solution : Given : $w_t = 40$ kg, density = 8000 kg/m^2, a = 200 J/m^2, f = 50 Hz

Volume of the specimen = $\dfrac{Wt}{density} = \dfrac{40}{8000} = 0.005$ m^3

$\therefore$ Hysteresis loss (W_h) = $200 \times 0.005 = 1$ J   ... (1)

Also, $W_h = A \cdot f$

At 60 Hz the hysteresis loss is given by

$$W_h = A \times 60 \qquad\qquad ...(2)$$

From equation (1) and (2)

$\therefore$ $60 \, A = 1$

$\therefore$ $A = \dfrac{1}{60}$

At 50 Hz, the hysteresis loss is given by,

$$W_h = Af$$

$\therefore$ $W_{h(50)} = A \times 50$

$$= \dfrac{1}{60} \times 50 = 0.833 \text{ J}$$

Example 3.3 : In an iron specimen hysteresis loss is 300 W when maximum flux density B_{max} is 0.9 Wb/m^2 and frequency is 50 Hz. What would be hysteresis loss if B_{max} is increased to 1.1 Wb/m^2 and frequency decreased to 40 Hz. Assume that hysteresis loss is proportional to $(B_{max})^{1.7}$

Solution :Given $P_{h(50)} = 300$, $B_{max(40)} = 1.1$ Wb/m^2 $B_{max(50)} = 0.9$ Wb/m^2

Hysteresis loss, $\qquad\qquad\qquad P_h \propto (B_{max})^{1.7} \cdot f$

At 50 Hz, $\qquad\qquad\qquad P_{h(50)} \propto (0.9)^{1.7} \times 50$

$\therefore \qquad\qquad\qquad\qquad 300 \propto (0.9)^{1.7} \times 50 \qquad\qquad\qquad\qquad\qquad ... (1)$

At 40 Hz,

$\qquad\qquad\qquad\qquad P_{h(40)} \propto (1.1)^{1.7} \times 40 \qquad\qquad\qquad\qquad\qquad ... (2)$

From equations (1) and (2),

$$\frac{P_{h(40)}}{P_{h(50)}} = \left(\frac{1.1}{0.9}\right)^{1.7} \times \left(\frac{40}{50}\right)$$

$$\therefore \qquad P_{h(40)} = \left(\frac{1.1}{0.9}\right)^{1.7} \times \left(\frac{40}{50}\right) \times 300$$

$$\therefore \qquad P_{h(40)} = 337.57 \text{ watts}$$

Example 3.4 : The core of transformer has an iron loss of 100 W at 40 Hz and 70 W at 30 Hz. Find the hysteresis loss at 50 Hz.

Solution : $\qquad\qquad\qquad\qquad P_h = $ Hysteresis loss $= A \cdot f$

$\qquad\qquad\qquad\qquad\qquad P_e = $ Eddy current loss

$\qquad\qquad\qquad\qquad\qquad P_e = B \cdot f^2$ (where, A and B are constants.)

$\therefore \qquad\qquad$ Iron loss, $P_i = P_h + P_e$

$\qquad\qquad\qquad\qquad\qquad P_i = A \cdot f + B \cdot f^2$

At 40 Hz,

$\qquad\qquad\qquad\qquad 100 = 40A + (40)^2 \, B$

$\therefore \qquad\qquad\qquad\qquad 100 = 40A + 1600 \, B$

$\therefore \qquad\qquad\qquad A + 40 \, B = 2.5 \qquad\qquad\qquad\qquad\qquad\qquad ... (1)$

At 30 Hz,

$\qquad\qquad\qquad\qquad 70 = 30A + (30)^2 \cdot B$

$\therefore \qquad\qquad\qquad\qquad 70 = 30 A + 900 \, B$

$\therefore \qquad\qquad\qquad 3 A + 90 \, B = 7 \qquad\qquad\qquad\qquad\qquad\qquad ... (2)$

Solving equations (1) and (2), we get : $A = \dfrac{11}{6}$, $B = \dfrac{1}{60}$

$$\therefore \ \text{Hysteresis loss at 50 Hz} = A \cdot f = \frac{11}{6} \times 50$$

$$= 91.67 \text{ watts}$$

Example 3.5 : The magnetic field in a piece of copper and another piece of Fe_2O_3 is 10^6 A/m. Their magnetic susceptibilities are -0.5×10^{-5} and 1.4×10^{-3} respectively. Compare the flux density and magnetization in the two pieces.

Solution : We know that, $B = \mu_0 \, \mu_r \, H$

$$\text{and} \qquad\qquad\qquad M = \chi_m \cdot H$$

$\therefore$ For copper, $\qquad\qquad B_{cu} = \mu_0 \cdot \mu_{rcu} \cdot H_{cu}$

and, $\qquad\qquad\qquad\qquad M_{cu} = \chi_{mcu} H_{cu}$

But, $\qquad\qquad\qquad\qquad \chi_{mcu} = \mu_{rcu} - 1$

$\therefore \qquad\qquad -0.5 \times 10^{-5} = \mu_{rcu} - 1$

$\therefore \qquad\qquad\qquad \mu_{rcu} = 1 - 0.5 \times 10^{-5}$

$\therefore \qquad\qquad\qquad B_{cu} = \mu_0 (1 - 0.5 \times 10^{-5}) \times 10^6 \qquad\qquad \text{... (1)}$

Similarly, $\qquad\qquad B_{fe2O3} = \mu_0 (1 + 1.4 \times 10^{-3}) \times 10^6 \qquad\qquad \text{... (2)}$

From equations (1) and (2),

$$\therefore \qquad \frac{B_{cu}}{B_{fe2O3}} = \frac{\mu_0 (1 - 0.5 \times 10^{-5}) \times 10^6}{\mu_0 (1 + 1.4 \times 10^{-3}) \times 10^6}$$

$$= \frac{1 - 0.5 \times 10^{-5}}{1 + 1.4 \times 10^{-3}}$$

$$= \frac{0.9999}{1.0014}$$

$$\therefore \qquad \frac{B_{cu}}{B_{fe2O3}} = 0.9985$$

Also, $M_{cu} = \chi_{mcu} \cdot H_{cu} = -0.5 \times 10^{-5} \times 10^6$

$$M_{cu} = -5 \qquad\qquad\qquad\qquad \text{... (3)}$$

$$M_{fe2O3} = 1.4 \times 10^{-3} \times 10^6$$

$$M_{fe2O3} = 1.4 \times 10^3 \qquad\qquad\qquad \text{... (4)}$$

From equations (3) and (4),

$$\frac{M_{cu}}{M_{fe2O3}} = \frac{-5}{1.4 \times 10^3}$$

$$\therefore \qquad \frac{M_{cu}}{M_{fe2O3}} = 3.5714 \times 10^{-3}$$

Example 3.6 : In a certain transformer the hysteresis loss was 160 W when maximum flux density was 1.1 Wb/m^2 and the supply frequency 60 Hz. What will be the hysteresis loss of the transformer when maximum flux density is reduced to 1.05 Wb/m^2 and supply frequency as 50 Hz. Assume hysteresis loss is given by $W_h \propto f \cdot B^{1.6}_m$ where f is supply frequency and B_{max} is maximum flux density.

Solution : Given : $B_{m(60)} = 1.1$, $W_{h(60)} = 160$, $B_{m(50)} = 1.05$, $W_{h(50)} = ?$

At 60 Hz, hysteresis loss is,

$$W_{h(60)} \quad \propto \quad 60\,(1.1)^{1.6} \qquad\qquad \text{... (1)}$$

At 50 Hz, hysteresis loss is,

$$W_{h(50)} \quad \propto \quad 50\,(1.05)^{1.6} \qquad\qquad \text{... (2)}$$

From (1),

$$\therefore \qquad\qquad W_{h(60)} \quad = \quad K \cdot 60\,(1.1)^{1.6}$$

$$\therefore \qquad\qquad 160 \quad = \quad K \cdot 60\,(1.1)^{1.6}$$

$$K \quad = \quad 2.29$$

$\therefore$ From (2),

$$W_{h(50)} \quad = \quad K \times 50\,(1.05)^{1.6}$$

$$= \quad 2.29 \times 50\,(1.05)^{1.6}$$

$$\therefore \qquad\qquad W_{h(50)} \quad = \quad 123.77 \text{ Watts}$$

Example 3.7 : In a material an application of magnetic field of 1.75×10^5 A/m causes a magnetic flux density of 0.2182 Wb/m^2. Calculate its permeability and susceptibility. Also find magnetization.

Soution : Given B=0.2182 Wb/m^2, H=1.75×10^5 A/m

$$B \quad = \quad \mu_0\,\mu_r\,H$$

$$0.2182 \quad = \quad 4\pi \times 10^{-7} \times \mu\,r \times 1.75 \times 10^5$$

$$\therefore \qquad\qquad \mu_r \quad = \quad \frac{0.2182}{4\pi \times 1.75 \times 10^{-2}}$$

$$\therefore \qquad\qquad \mu_r \quad = \quad 0.9922$$

Now, $\qquad\qquad \mu \quad = \quad \mu_0\,\mu_r$

$$= \quad 4\pi \times 10^{-7} \times 0.9922$$

$$\mu \quad = \quad 12.468 \times 10^{-7}$$

$$\therefore \qquad\qquad \chi_m \quad = \quad \mu_r - 1$$

$$= \quad 0.9922 - 1$$

$$\therefore \qquad\qquad \chi_m \quad = \quad -7.8 \times 10^{-3}$$

Now, $M = \chi_m \cdot H$

$= -7.8 \times 10^{-3} \times 1.75 \times 10^5$

$\therefore$ $M = -13.65 \times 10^2$

$\therefore$ $M = -1365$ A/m

Example 3.8 : The total loss in a sample of sheet steel to be used for transformer core at 50 Hz and 75 Hz are 20 watts and 35 watts respectively both having been measured at the same peak flux density. Separate the losses at 50 Hz into its hysteresis and eddy current components.

Solution : We have, $Pi = Af + Bf^2$

$\therefore$ Total loss at 50 Hz,

$20 = Af + B \cdot f^2$

$= A \times 50 + B \times (50)^2$

$20 = 50\,A + 2500\,B$

$\therefore$ $A + 50\,B = 0.4$ ... (1)

Total loss at 75 Hz,

$\therefore$ $35 = Af + Bf2$

$35 = 75\,A + B \cdot (75)2$

$\therefore$ $A + 75\,B = 0.47$ ... (2)

Solving equations (1) and (2), we get,

$25\,B = 0.07$

$\therefore$ $\boxed{B = 0.0028}$

Putting this in equation (1),

$\therefore$ $A + 50 \times 0.0028 = 0.4$

$\therefore$ $\boxed{A = 0.26}$

$\therefore$ Hysteresis loss $= Af$

$= 0.26 \times 50 = 13$ Watts

$\therefore$ Eddy current loss $= Bf2$

$= 0.0028 \times (50)^2 = 7$ Watts

Example 3.9 : Calculate hysteresis loss is a specimen of iron subjected to magnetization of 50 Hz. The weight of specimen is 40 kg and its density is 7680 kg/m^3. The hysteresis loop area is equivalent to 198 J/m^3.

Solution :   **Given :** $w_t = 40$ kg, density = 7680 kg/m^2, $f = 50$ Hz

$$\text{Volume of specimen} \quad = \frac{40}{7680} \text{ m}^3$$

$$= 5.2083 \times 10^{-3} \text{ m}^3$$

$\therefore$ Hysteresis loss at 50 Hz = Volume × Loop area = $\left[\dfrac{40}{7680}\right] \times 198 = 1.03$ Joules

---

Example 3.10 : Give expression for hysteresis loss. The hysteresis loss for a given material is 1.55 watts per kg at 50 Hz, with maximum flux density of 1 Wb/m². Its specific gravity is 7.75. A core of this material is to be used, which will be subjected to 60 Hz and maximum flux density of 7.9 Wb/m². The volume of core is 980 cm³. Determine :

- The value of hysteresis loss constant in the above expression.
- The hysteresis loss in the core at 60 Hz.

Assume that the hysteresis loss is proportional to $B_{max}^{1.6}$ where, B_{max} is maximum flux density in the core.

Solution : Hysteresis loss, $\quad W_h \quad = \quad K \cdot B_{max}^{1.6} \cdot f$

Hysteresis loss at 50 Hz,

$$W_h \quad = \quad 1.55 \text{ Watts/kg}$$

$\therefore \qquad\qquad\qquad \text{Mass} \quad = \quad \dfrac{\text{Volume of core} \times \text{Specific gravity}}{1000} \text{ kg}$

$$= \quad \frac{980 \times 7.75}{1000} \text{ kg}$$

$$\text{Mass} \quad = \quad 7.595 \text{ kg}$$

$\therefore$ Total hysteresis loss W_h at 50 Hz

$$W_h \quad = \quad 1.55 \times 7.595$$

$\therefore \qquad\qquad\qquad\quad W_h \quad = \quad 11.772 \text{ watts}$

Also, $\qquad\qquad\qquad\quad W_h \quad = \quad K \cdot B_{max}^{1.6} \cdot f \quad \text{... at 50 Hz}$

$\therefore \qquad\qquad\quad 11.772 \quad = \quad K\,(1)^{1.6} \times 50$

$\therefore \qquad\qquad\qquad\quad K \quad = \quad 0.2354$

Now, Hysteresis loss, W_h at 60 Hz is

$$W_{h(60)} \quad = \quad K \cdot B_{max}^{1.6} \cdot f$$

$$= \quad (0.2354) \cdot (7.9)^{1.6} \times 60$$

$$W_{h(60)} \quad = \quad 385.58 \text{ Watts}$$

Example 3.11 : In a magnetic material the field strength was found to be 10^6 Amp/m. If the magnetic susceptibility of the material is -0.5×10^{-5}. Calculate magnetization and flux density in the material.

Solution : Given : $H = 10^6$ Amp/m, $\chi_m = -0.5 \times 10^{-5}$, $M = ?$, $B = ?$

$$\because \qquad M = \chi_m \times H$$
$$= -0.5 \times 10^{-5} \times 10^6$$
$$\therefore \qquad M = -0.5 \times 10$$
$$\therefore \qquad M = -5$$

Also,
$$\chi_m = \mu_r - 1$$
$$\therefore \qquad \mu_r = \chi_m + 1$$
$$= (-0.5 \times 10^{-5}) + 1$$
$$\therefore \qquad \mu_r = 0.9999$$

Now,
$$B = \mu_0 \mu_r H$$
$$= 4\pi \times 10^{-7} \times 0.9999 \times 10^6$$
$$\therefore \qquad B = 1.2566 \text{ Wb/m}^2$$

Example 3.12 : In a certain transformer the hysteresis loss was formed to be 160 watt when maximum flux density was 1.1 Wb/m^2 and supply frequency 60 Hz. What will be the hysteresis loss of the transformer when the maximum flux density is reduced to 0.9 Wb/m^2 and the supply frequency to 50 Hz? Assume hysteresis loss is given by $W_h \propto f\, B_{max}^{1.6}$ where, f is frequency in Hz and B_{max} is maximum flux density.

Solution : Given : $P_h = 160$ W, $B_m = 1.1$ T, $f = 60$ Hz, $P_{h(new)} = ?$, $B_{m(new)} = 0.9$ T, $f_{new} = 50$ Hz

Since hysteresis loss, $\qquad P_h \propto f B_m^{1.6}$

$\therefore$ At 60 Hz hysteresis loss is $160 \propto 60 \times (1.1)^{1.6}$ ... (1)

At 50 Hz hysteresis loss is $P_{h(new)} \propto 50(0.9)^{1.6}$ ... (2)

From equation (1),

$$160 = K\, 60 \times (1.1)^{1.6}$$
$$\therefore \qquad K = \frac{160}{60 \times (1.1)^{1.6}}$$
$$\therefore \qquad K = 2.2894$$

Putting this value of K in equation (2),

$$\therefore \qquad P_{h(new)} = K \cdot 50 \times (0.9)1.6$$
$$= (2.2894) \times 50 \times (0.9)1.6$$
$$\therefore \qquad Ph(new) = 96.71 \text{ watts}$$

Example 3.13 : In a certain transformer the hysteresis loss is 300 watts when the maximum flux density is 0.9 Wb/m^2 and the frequency 50 Hz. What would be the hysteresis loss if the maximum flux density were increased to 1.1 Wb/m^2 and the frequency 40 Hz. Assume the hysteresis loss over this range to be proportional to $B_{max}^{1.7}$.

Solution : **Given :** P_h = 300 W, B_{max} = 0.9 T, f = 50 Hz, $P_{h\,(new)}$ = ?, $B_{m\,(new)}$ = 1.1 T, $f_{(new)}$ = 40 Hz.

Since $\qquad\qquad\qquad\qquad P_h \propto f\,B_m^{1.7}$

At 50 Hz, $\qquad\qquad\qquad 300 \propto 50 \times (0.9)^{1.7}$ $\qquad\qquad\qquad\qquad$ ... (1)

At 40 Hz, $\qquad\qquad\quad P_{n\,(new)} \propto 40 \times (1.1)^{1.7}$ $\qquad\qquad\qquad\qquad$ ... (2)

From eqatuion (1)

$$300 = K \cdot 50 \times (0.9)^{1.7}$$

$\therefore \qquad\qquad\qquad\qquad K = \dfrac{300}{50 \times (0.9)^{1.7}}$

$$K = 7.1769$$

Putting this value of K in Equation (2), we get;

$$P_{h\,(new)} = K \cdot 40 \times (1.1)^{1.7}$$
$$= (7.1769) \times 40\,(1.1)^{1.7}$$
$$P_{h\,(new)} = 337.57 \text{ Watts}$$

Example 3.14 : Calculate hysteresis loss in iron specimen subjected to magnetization of 50 Hz. The weight of specimen is 50 kg and density is 8000 kg/m^3. The hysteresis loop area is equivalent to 250 J/m^3.

Solution   **Given :** w_t = 40 kg, density = 8000 kg/m^2, f = 50 Hz

$$\text{Volume} = \frac{\text{Weight}}{\text{Density}}$$

$$= \frac{50 \text{ kg}}{8000 \text{ kg/m}^3}$$

$$= 6.25 \times 10^{-3} \text{ m}^3$$

$\therefore \qquad$ Hysteresis loss $= $ Volume $\times$ Area of hysteresis loop

$$= \left(\frac{50}{8000}\right) \times 250 = 1.5625 \text{ Joules}$$

Example 3.15 : Calculate loss of energy caused by hysteresis in one hour in 50 kg of iron, if peak flux density is 1.3 T and frequency is 25 Hz. Assume Stenmetz coefficient 628 J/m^3 and density of iron 7.5×10^3 kg/m^3.

Solution : $\qquad\qquad$ Volume of iron $= \dfrac{\text{Weight}}{\text{Density}}$

$$= \frac{50}{7.5 \times 10^3}$$

$$= 6.6 \times 10^{-3} \ m^3$$

Hysteresis loss, P_h = $K_h \cdot B_m^{16} \cdot fv$

$$= 628 \times (1.3)^{1.6} \times 25 \times 6.6 \times 10^{-3}$$

∴   Loss of energy due to hysteresis in 1 hr. is

$$= 159.26 \times 60 \times 60 \ \text{watt sec.}$$

$$= 573.33 \times 10^3 \ \text{watt sec. or Joules.}$$

Example 3.16 : A magnetic field strength of Fe_2O_3 is 10^6 Amp/m. Given that magnetic susceptibility of Fe_2O_3 at room temperature is 1.25×10^{-3}. Calculate induced magnetization, flux density and permeability.

Solution : Given $\chi_m = 1.25 \times 10^{-3}, H = 10^6$ Amp/m

$$\chi_m = \frac{M}{H}$$

∴ M = $\chi_m \cdot H$

$$= 1.25 \times 10^{-3} \times 10^6$$

∴ M = 1.25×10^3

Also, χ_m = $\mu_r - 1$

∴ μ_r = $\chi_m + 1$

$$= (1.25 \times 10^{-3}) + 1$$

∴ μ_r = 1.00125

Since, B = $\mu_0 \mu_r H$

$$= 4\pi \times 10^{-7} \times 1.00125 \times 10^6$$

∴ B = $1.2582 \ Wb/m^2$

∴   Permeability, μ = B/H

$$= \frac{1.2582}{10^{-6}}$$

$$= 1.2582 \times 10^{-6}$$

Example 3.17 : In a certain transformer the hysteresis loss is 400 W when maximum flux density is 0.85 Wb/m^2 and frequency of 50 Hz. What would be the hysteresis loss if maximum flux density is increased to 1.4 Wb/m^2 and frequency to 60 Hz. Assume hysteresis loss over this range is to be proportional to $B_m^{1.7}$.

Solution : Given : P_h = 400 W, B_m = 0.85 T, f = 50 Hz, $P_{h(new)}$ = ?, $B_{m(new)}$ = 1.4 T, $f_{(new)}$ = 60 Hz.

Since hysteresis loss, $P_h \propto B_m^{1.7} f$

∴ At 50 Hz, $P_h \propto (0.85)^{1.7} \times 50$

∴ $400 = K \cdot (0.85)^{1.7} \times 50$

∴ $K = \dfrac{400}{(0.85)^{1.7} \times 50}$

∴ $K = 10.5457$

Now, at 60 Hz,

$P_{h(new)} \propto (1.4)^{1.7} \times 60$

∴ $P_{h(new)} = K \cdot (1.4)^{1.7} \times 60$

∴ $P_{h(new)} = (10.5457)(1.4)^{1.7} \times 60$

∴ $P_{h(new)} = 1121.09$ watts

Example 3.18 : Find the power loss in watts due to hysteresis only for an iron core of volume 100 cm^3 which is subjected to 50 cycles of magnetization per sec. The hysteresis loop for the core has an area of 150 cm^2 when plotted to scales of 1 cm = 0.2 T and 1 cm = 500 A/m.

Solution : Given a=150 cm^2,f=50Hz

Hysteresis loop area $= 150$ cm^2

∴   Loss $= xy$ J/m^3/cycle

$= 0.2 \times 500$

$= 100$ J/m^3/cycle

∴ $W_h =$ Hysteresis loss

$= 100 \times 100 \times 10^{-4} \times 50$

∴ $W_h = 50$ watts

Example 3.19 : Calculate hysteresis loss in a specimen of iron subjected to a magnetization of 60 Hz. The weight of specimen is 50 kg and its density is 8000 kg/m^3. Hysteresis loop area is equivalent to 250 J/m^3. What will be the hysteresis loss of specimen at 40 Hz?

Solution : Given : w_t = 50 kg, density = 8000 kg/m^2, f = 60 Hz

$$\text{Volume of specimen} = \frac{560}{8000} = 6.25 \times 10^{-3} \, m^3$$

Hysteresis loss, W_h = $250 \times 6.25 \times 10^{-3}$

$\quad$ = 1.5625 Joules   ... (1)

Also, W_h = $A \cdot f = A \times 60$ ... (2)

From equations (1) and (2),

$\quad$ 60 A = 1.5625

∴   A = 0.02604

At 40 Hz,

$\quad$ $W_{h(40)}$ = $A \cdot f$

$\quad$ = $(0.02604) \times 40$

$\quad$ $W_{h(40)}$ = 1.04166 J

Example 3.20 : In a material, an application of magnetic field of 2.75×10^6 A/m causes a magnetic flux density of 0.2485 Wb/m^2. Calculate its permeability, susceptibility and magnetization.

Solution :   B = $\mu_0 \mu_r H$

$$\mu_r = \frac{B}{\mu_0 H} = \frac{0.2485}{4\pi \times 10^{-7} \times 2.75 \times 10^6}$$

$\quad$ μ_r = 0.07190

$\quad$ μ = $\mu_0 \mu_r = 4\pi \times 10^{-7} \times 0.07190$

$\quad$ μ = 0.9036×10^{-7}

Now, χ_m = $\mu_r - 1$

$\quad$ = 0.0719 − 1

$\quad$ χ_m = −0.9281

Now,   M = $\chi_m \cdot H$

$\quad$ = $(-0.9281) \times 2.75 \times 10^6$

∴   M = −2552275 A/m

Example 3.21 : The total loss in a silicon sheet used for transformer core at 50 Hz and 75 Hz are 20 watts and 35 watts respectively, both being measured at same peak flux density. Calculate its hysteresis loss and eddy current loss at 75 Hz.

Solution :

$$P_i = Af + Bf^2$$

At 50 Hz,

$$20 = 50A + 2500B$$

$$A + 50B = 0.4 \qquad \qquad ...(1)$$

At 75 Hz,

$$A + 75B = 0.47 \qquad \qquad ...(2)$$

Solving equations (1) and (2),

$$A = 0.26$$

At 75 Hz,

$$\therefore \qquad P_h = Af$$

$$= 0.26 \times 75$$

$$= 19.5 \text{ watt}$$

$$P_e = Bf^2$$

$$= 0.0028 \times (75)^2$$

$$= 15.75 \text{ watt}$$

Example 3.22 : Calculate loss of energy caused by hysteresis in two hours in 50 kg of iron if peak flux density is 1.3 T and frequency is 75 Hz. Assume the Stenmetz coefficient 628 J/m^3 and density of iron as $7.5 \times 10^3 \text{ kg/m}^3$.

Solution : Given : w_t = 50 kg, density = 7500 kg/m^2, f = 75 Hz

Volume of iron

$$= \frac{\text{Weight}}{\text{Density}}$$

$$= \frac{50}{7.5 \times 10^3}$$

$$= 6.6 \times 10^{-3}$$

Hysteresis loss $= P_h = K_h B_m^{1.6} fv$

$$P_h = 477.78 \text{ watt}$$

Loss and energy due to P_h in 2 hours = $477.78 \times 2 \times 60 \times 60$

$$= 3440016 \text{ watt-sec. or Joules}$$

Example 3.23 : In a certain transformer the hysteresis loss is 500 W when the maximum flux density is 0.78 tesla and frequency is 40 Hz. What would be the hysteresis loss if maximum flux density is increased to 1.6 tesla and frequency is 70 Hz? Assume hysteresis loss over this range is to be proportional to $B_m^{1.7}$.

Solution : Hysteresis loss $\qquad P_h \propto (B_m)^{1.7} \cdot f$

At 40 Hz, $P_{h(40)} \propto (0.78)^{1.7} \times 40$ ... (1)

At 70 Hz, $P_{h(70)} \propto (1.6)^{1.7} \times 70$ ... (2)

From equations (1) and (2),

$$\frac{P_{h(40)}}{P_{h(70)}} = \left(\frac{0.78}{1.6}\right)^{1.7} \times \frac{40}{70}$$

$$\frac{500}{P_{h(70)}} = 0.5714$$

∴ $$P_{h(70)} = \frac{500}{0.1684}$$

∴ $$P_{h(70)} = 2969.12 \text{ Watts}$$

Example 3.24 : Calculate hysteresis loss in a specimen of iron subjected to magnetization at 50 Hz. The weight of the specimen is 70 kg and its density is 7680 kg/m^3. The hysteresis loop area is equivalent to 300 J/m^3.

Solution : Given : w_t = 70 kg, density = 7680 kg/m^2, f = 50 Hz

Volume of specimen $= \dfrac{70}{7680} \text{ m}^3$

                              $= 9.1146 \times 10^{-3} \text{ m}^3$

Hysteresis loss at 50 Hz   = Volume × Loop area

                              $= 9.1146 \times 10^{-3} \times 300$

                              = 2.734 Joules

Example 3.25 : Calculate Hysteresis loss in a specimen of iron subjected to a magnetization of 60 Hz. The weight of specimen is 50 kg and its density is 8000 kg/m^3. Hysteresis loop area is equivalent 250 J/m^3. What will be hysteresis loss of specimen of 40 Hz?

Solution : Given : w_t = 50 kg, density = 8000 kg/m^2, f = 60 Hz

Volume of specimen $= \dfrac{\text{Weight}}{\text{Density}}$

                        $= \dfrac{50}{8000}$

                        $= 6.25 \times 10^{-3} \text{ m}^3$

Hysteresis loss (W_h) $= 250 \times 6.25 \times 10^{-3}$

                        $W_h = 1.56$ Joules

Now, $W_h = A \cdot f$

                        $= A \times 60$

$$1.56 \ = \ 60\,A$$

$$A \ = \ 1/60$$

At 40 Hz, hysteresis loss is given by,

$$W_h \ = \ A \times f$$

$$W_h \ = \ \frac{1}{60} \times 40$$

$$W_h \ = \ 0.66 \text{ Joules}$$

QUESTIONS

1. Short note on

    (i)   Diamagnetism

    (ii) Paramagnetism

    (iii) Ferromagnetism

    (iv) Anti-Ferromagnetism

    (v)   Ferrimagnetism

2. Explain application of magnetic materials.

3. Explain magnetic dipole moment.

4. What is relative permeability and magnetic susceptibility ?

5. Give classification of magnetic materials.

6. What magnetic properties are required for the magnetic materials used in

    (a) Power transformer

    (b) Memory disc of a computer

7. What is ferrites name some ferrites and give their applications.

8. What are ferrites? Name some ferrites and give their applications.

9. Explain the terms

    (a) Permeability   (b)   Magnetic susceptibility

    (c) Magnetization   (d)   Magnetic dipole

10. Differentiate between

    (a) Soft and hard magnetic material.

    (b) Ferromagnetism and ferrimagnetism.

11. Explain

    (a) Magnetization

    (b) Susceptibility

12. List the properties and type of magnetic materials required for

    (a) Power transformer

    (b) D.C. shunt generator

13. Explain

    (a) Ferromagnetic domain

    (b) Spontaneous magnetization

14. From the basics' prove that $B = \mu_o (H + M)$

15. Explain

    (a) Magnetic dipole moment

    (b) Magnetic susceptibility

    (c) Permeability

    (d) Flux density

16. Draw the hysteresis loop of ferromagnetic material and explain the following

    (a) Coersive force

    (b) Residual magnetism

17. Classify magnetic material explain each class with respect to its properties and applications.

18. What are ferrites? Give their properties and applications.

19. Define relative permeability. Show that the relative permeability $\mu_r = 1 + x_m$ where, x_m is magnetic susceptibility.

20. Explain classification of magnetic material on the basis of distribution of dipole moment.

21. What is Curie temperature for ferromagnetic material? Describe Curie Weiss law.

22. Differentiate between

    (a) Soft and hard magnetic material.

    (b) Ferromagnetism of antiferromagnetism.

23. Define the following

    (a) Permeability

    (b) Magnetic dipole moment

    (c) Magnetic susceptibility

    (d) Magnetization

24. What are soft and hard magnetic materials? Give their characteristics and applications?

25. Differentiate between

    (a) Magnetic dipole moment and electric dipole moment.

    (b) Ferromagnetism and antiferromagnetism.

26. Classify the magnetic material and explain each class with respect to its properties and applications.

27. Calculate hysteresis loss in a specimen of iron subjected to a magnetisation of 60 Hz. The weight of specimen is 50 kg and its density is 8000 kg/m^3. Hysteresis loop area is equivalent to 250 J/m^3. What will be the hysteresis loss of specimen at 40 Hz?

28. In a material an application of magnetic field of 2.75×10^6 A/m causes a magnetic flux density of 0.2485 Wb/m^2. Calculate its permeability, susceptibility and magnetization.

29. Explain spontaneous magnetization and Curie Weiss law.

30. Write a short note on magnetic recording materials and compact discs.

31. Describe properties and applications of paramagnetic materials.

32. Differentiate between

    (a) Permeability and magnetic susceptibility.

    (b) Soft and hard magnetic materials.

33. Explain the terms

    (i)   Permeability

    (ii) Magnetisation

    (iii) Curie temperature

    (iv) Magnetic susceptibility

34. State properties and applications of Hard magnetic materials.

35. Classify magnetic materials based on dipole moment. Explain each class with respect to its properties and applications.

36. Write a note on behavior of ferromagnetic materials below critical temperature.

37. The total loss in a silicon sheet used for transformer core at 50 Hz and 75 Hz are 20 watts and 35 watts respectively, both being measured at same peak flux density. Calculate its hysteresis loss and eddy current loss at 75 Hz.

38. Calculate loss of energy caused by hysteresis in two hours in 50 kg of iron if peak flux density is 1.3 T and frequency is 75 Hz. Assume the Stenmetz coefficient 628 J/m^3 and density of iron as 7.5×10^3 kg/m^3.

39. Explain classification of magnetic materials on the basis of distribution of dipole components. Give applications of each class.

40. Differentiate between

    (i)   Soft and hard magnetic materials.

    (ii) Permeability and magnetic susceptibility.

41. What is Currie temperature for ferromagnetic material? Explain spontaneous magnetization and Curie-Weiss law.

42. Write short notes on

    (i)   Magnetic recording materials.

    (ii) Compact discs.

43. Explain Curie-Weiss law for ferromagnetic materials. Is this law application for spontaneous magnetization? Hence explain spontaneous magnetization.

44. What are Ferrites? Give properties and applications of ferrites.

45. Explain classification of magnetic materials on the basis of distribution of magnetic dipole moments.

46. Write short notes on

    (i) Compact Disc

    (ii) Magnetic Recording Materials

47. In a certain transformer the hysteresis loss is 500 W when the maximum flux density is 0.78 tesla and frequency is 40 Hz. What would be the hysteresis loss if maximum flux density is increased to 1.6 tesla and frequency is 70 Hz? Assume hysteresis loss over this range is to be proportional to $B_m^{1.7}$.

48. Calculate hysteresis loss in a specimen of iron subjected to magnetization of 50 Hz. The weight of the specimen is 70 kg and its density is 7680 kg/m^3. The hysteresis loop area is equivalent to 300 J/m^3.

49. Differentiate between Soft Magnetic Materials and Hard Magnetic Materials.

50. Explain the properties and applications Diamagnetism, Para-magnetism, Ferro magnetism and Ferrimagnetism.

51. Calculate hysteresis loss in a specimen of iron subjected to a magnetization of 60 Hz. The weight of specimen is 50 kg and its density is 8000 kg/m^3. Hysteresis loop area is equivalent 250 J/m^3. What will be hysteresis loss of specimen of 40 Hz?

✠ ✠ ✠

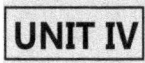

DIELECTRICS

4.1 INTRODUCTION

Every material in the world can be defined in terms of how it conducts electricity. Certain things, such as cold glass, do not conduct electricity. They are known as insulators. Materials which do conduct electricity, like copper, aluminum are called conductors. In the middle are materials known as semiconductors, which do not conduct as well as conductors, but can carry current. such materials called superconductors, which when brought down to very low temperatures turn into superhighways of current, they conduct electricity without any resistance.

4.2 A DIELECTRIC MATERIAL

A dielectric material is an electrical insulator that can be polarized by an applied electric field.

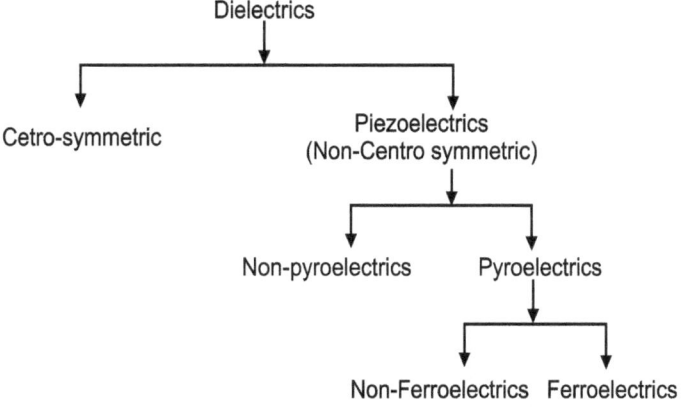

Fig. 4.1

When a dielectric is placed in an electric field, electric charges do not flow through the material as they do in a conductor, but cause dielectric polarization. Because of dielectric polarization, positive charges are displaced toward the field and negative charges shift in the opposite direction. This creates an internal electric field that reduces the overall field within the dielectric. The study of dielectric properties concerns storage and dissipation of electric as well as magnetic energy in materials. It is important to explain various phenomena in electronics, optics, and solid-state physics.

Dielectric Constant : The dielectric constant is the ratio of the permittivity of a substance to the permittivity of free space. It is an electrical equivalent of relative magnetic permeability. As the dielectric constant increases, the electric flux density increases, if all other factors remain unchanged. This enables objects of a given size, such as sets of metal plates, to hold their electric charge for long periods of time, and/or to hold large quantities of charge. Materials with high dielectric constants are mainly useful in the manufacture of high-value capacitors.

Electric permittivity, is a constant of proportionality that exists between electric displacement and electric field intensity. This constant is equal to approximately 8.85×10^{-12} farad per meter (F/m) in free space. In other materials, it can be much different, often substantially greater than the free-space value, which is symbolized ε_0. In engineering applications, permittivity is often expressed in relative, rather than in absolute permittivity. If ε_0 represents the permittivity of free space (that is 8.85×10^{-12} F/m) and ε represents the permittivity of the substance in question (also specified in farads per metre), then the relative permittivity, also called the dielectric constant ε_r, is given by

$$\varepsilon_r = \varepsilon/\varepsilon_0$$
$$= \varepsilon (1.13 \times 10^{11})$$

Various substances have dielectric constants ε_r greater than 1. These substances are generally called dielectric materials, or dielectrics. Commonly used dielectrics include glass, various ceramics, paper, mica, polyethylene, and certain metal oxides. Dielectrics are used in capacitors and transmission lines in Alternating Current (AC), Audio Frequency (AF), and radio frequency (RF) applications.

Dipole Moment

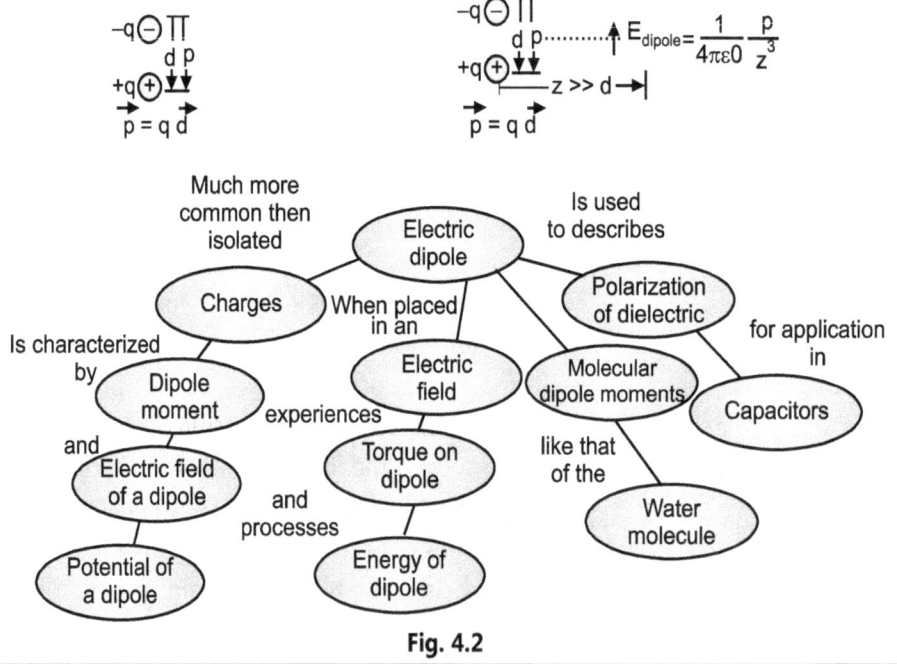

Fig. 4.2

The electric dipole moment for a pair of opposite charges of magnitude q is defined as the magnitude of the charge times the distance between them and the defined direction is toward the positive charge. It is a useful concept in atoms and molecules where the effects of charge separation are important, but the distances between the charges are too small to be easily measurable. It is also very useful concept in dielectrics and other applications in solid and liquid materials. Applications involve the electric field of a dipole and the energy of a dipole when placed in an electric field. As shown in below Fig. 4.2.

4.3 POLARIZATION

Polarization of Dielectric : If a material contains polar molecules, they will generally be in random orientations when no electric field is applied. An applied electric field by orienting the dipole moments of polar molecules which will polarize the material. This decreases the effective electric field between the plates and will increase the capacitance of the parallel plate structure. The dielectric must be a good electric insulator so as to minimize any DC leakage current through a capacitor.

The presence of the dielectric decreases by the electric field produced by a given charge density.

$$E_{effectuve} = E - E_{polarization} = \frac{\sigma}{k\varepsilon_o}$$

The factor k by which the effective field is decreased by the polarization of the dielectric is called the dielectric constant of the material.

Unpolarized

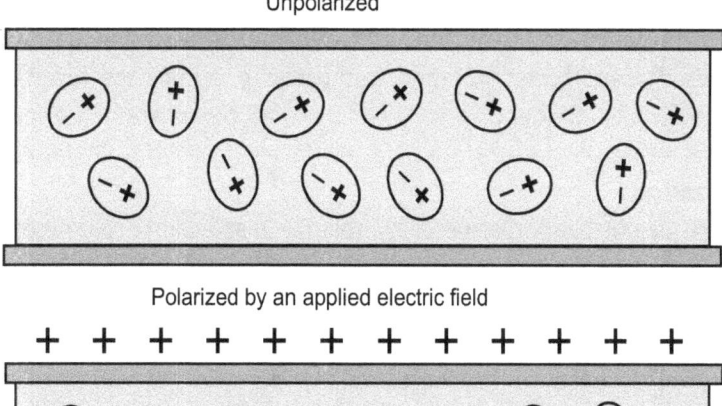

Polarized by an applied electric field

Fig. 4.3

4.3.1 Comparison between Polar Dielectric and Non-Polar Dielectric

Polar Dielectric	Non-polar Dielectric
1. The centres of positive and negative charges do not coincide because of the asymmetric shape of the molecules in Polar Dielectric	1. The centre of positive charge coincides with centre of negative charge in the molecule in Non-polar dielectric.
2. It has dipole moment in the application of external electric field.	2. It has very small dipole moment to each molecule in the application of external electric field.

4.3.2 Dielectric Polarization

(1) Dipolar Polarization

Dipolar polarization is a polarization that is either inherent to polar molecules which is orientation polarization, or can be induced in any molecule in which the asymmetric distortion of the nuclei is possible. Orientation polarization results from a permanent dipole. When an external electric field is applied, the distance between charges within each permanent dipole, which is related to chemical bonding, remains constant in orientation polarization. But in the direction of polarization it rotates. This rotation occurs on a timescale that depends on the torque and surrounding viscosity of the molecules. Because the rotation is not instantaneous, dipolar polarizations lose the response to electric fields at the highest frequencies. The delay of the response to the change of the electric field causes friction and heat. When an external electric field is applied at infrared frequencies or less than it, the molecules are bent and stretched by the field and the molecular dipole moment changes. The molecular vibration frequency is roughly the inverse of the time it takes for the molecules to bend, and this distortion polarization disappears above the infrared.

(2) Ionic Polarization

Ionic polarization is polarization caused by relative displacements between positive and negative ions in ionic crystals (for example, NaCl). If a crystal consists of atoms of more than one kind, the distribution of charges around an atom in the crystal or molecule leans to positive or negative. Because of this, when lattice vibrations or molecular vibrations induce relative displacements of the atoms, the centers of positive and negative charges are also displaced. The locations of these centers are affected by the symmetry of the displacements. When the centers don't correspond, polarizations arise in crystals. This polarization is called ionic polarization. Ionic polarization causes the ferroelectric effect as well as dipolar polarization. In the ferroelectric transition, which is caused by the lining up of the orientations of permanent dipoles along a particular direction, is called an order-disorder phase transition. The transition caused by ionic polarizations in crystals is called a displacive phase transition.

4.3.3 Piezoelectric Material

Piezoelectric Material that possesses the property of converting mechanical energy into electrical energy and vice versa.

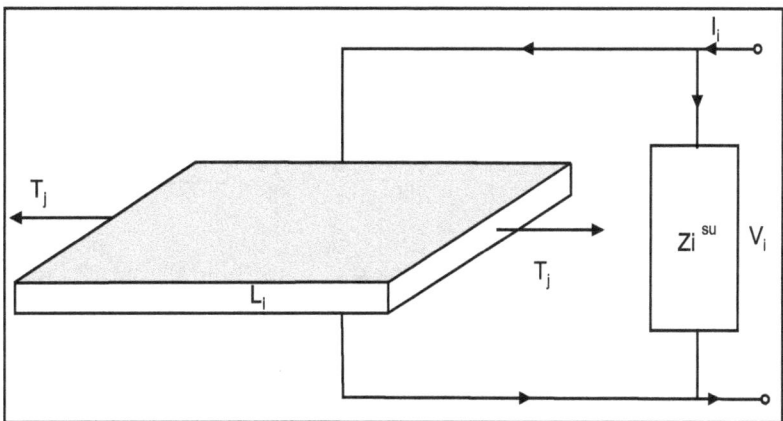

Fig. 4.4 : Piezoelectric materials

- It is reversible an applied mechanical stress will generate a voltage and an applied voltage will change the shape of the solid by a small amount (up to 4% change in volume).

- In physics, the piezoelectric effect can be described as the link between electrostatics and mechanics.

Direct Piezoelectric Effect

Piezoelectric material will generate electric potential when subjected to some kind of mechanical stress.

The Direct Effect : Strain sensor, gas lighters, microphones, ultrasonic detectors.

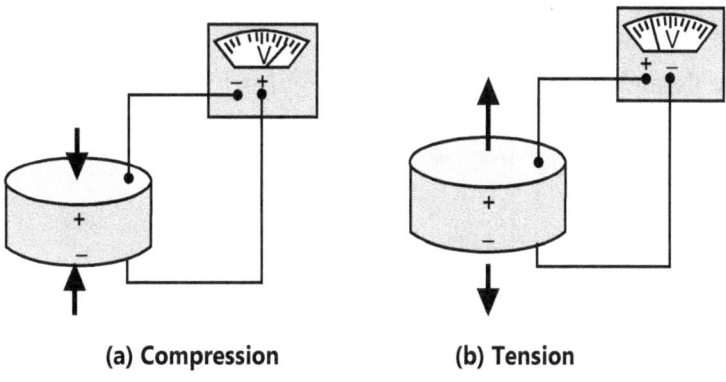

(a) Compression　　　　　**(b) Tension**

Fig. 4.5

Inverse Piezoelectric Effect : If the piezoelectric material is exposed to an electric field it consequently lengthens or shortens proportional to the voltage. E.g. Crystal oscillators, crystal speakers, record player pick ups, actuators etc.

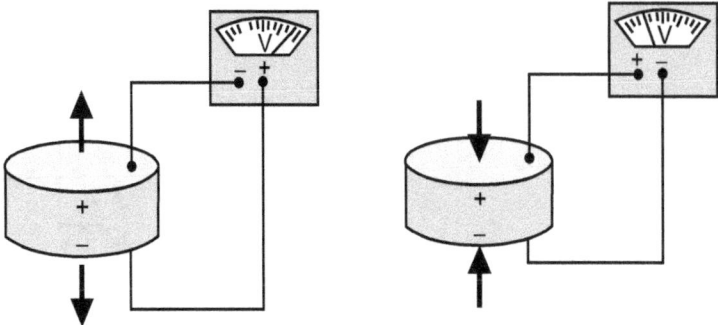

Fig. 4.6

The necessary condition for the piezoelectric effect is the absence of a center of symmetry in the crystal structure. For example: Of the 32 crystals classes 21 lack a center of symmetry, and with the exceptions of one class, all these are piezoelectric. If lead zirconate titanate (PZT), a piezoceramic, is placed between two electrodes and a pressure causing a reduction of only $1/20^{th}$ of one millimeter is applied, a 100,000 volt potential is produced.

The basic equations of piezoelectricity are

$$P = D \times stress$$

and

$$E = strain/D$$

Where,

P = Polarization

E = Electric field generated

D = Piezoelectric coefficient in metres per volt.

- **Naturally Occurring Crystals :** $AlPO_4$, Cane sugar, Quartz, Rochelle salt, Topaz, Tourmaline group minerals, and dry bone.

- **Man-Made Crystals :** Gallium orthophosphate ($GaPO_4$), Langasite ($La_3Ga_5SiO_{14}$).

- **Man-Made Ceramics :** Barium titanate ($BaTiO_3$), Lead titanate ($PbTiO_3$), Lead zirconate titanate ($Pb[Zr_x Ti_1] O_3$ $0 < x < 1$). More commonly known as PZT, Potassium niobate ($KNbO_3$), Lithium niobate ($LiNbO_3$) Lithium tantalate ($LiTaO_3$), Sodium tungstate ($NaxWO_3$).

- **Polymers :** Polyvinylidene fluoride (PVDF).

- **Pyroelectric Materials :** A special class of material which is subset of piezoelectric material. This are polarized spontaneously but they do not respond to an electric field like ferroelectronics require very high electric field for orienting the dipoles.

The field required for some materials is so high that the material reaches electric breakdown before it can get polarized. But when temperature is changed the polarization of crystal changes e.g. $LiNbO_3$.

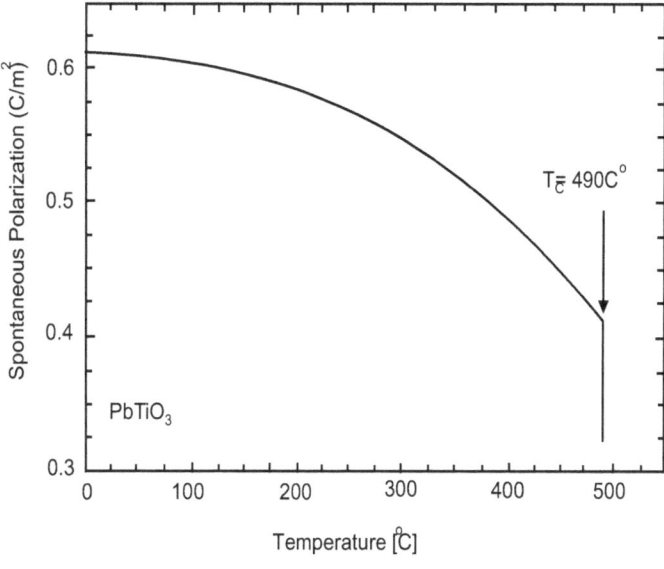

Fig. 4.7

The spontaneous polarization is strongly dependent on the temperature. It disappears completely at the phase transformation temperature T_c. The variation in the polarization effect with respect to the temperature is called the pyroelectric effect.

$$p = \left(\frac{dD}{dT}\right)_E = \frac{dP_s}{dT} + d\frac{de}{dT}$$

4.3.4 Ferroelectric

- Some ionic crystals and polymer dielectrics exhibit a spontaneous dipole moment, which can be reversed by an externally applied electric field. This is called the ferroelectric effect. These materials are similar to the ferromagnetic materials behave within an externally applied magnetic field. Ferroelectric materials often have very high dielectric constants, making them very useful for capacitors.

- Ferromagnetism was already known when ferroelectricity was discovered in 1920, in by Valasek. Thus, the prefix ferro, meaning iron, was used to describe the property despite the fact that most ferroelectric materials do not contain iron.

- All Ferroelectric materials exhibit Piezoelectric effect because of lack of symmetry.

- Special class of Piezoelectric material exhibit spontaneous polarization i.e., polarization in the absence of an electric field.

- Ferroelectrics are the electric analog of the ferromagnets, which may show permanent magnetic behaviour.
- Valasek discovered the first ferroelectric material, namely Rochelle salt.
- In ferroelectrics, the polarization can be varied and even reversed by an external electric field.

Properties

- Extremely high dielectric constant (~500 to 15,000).
- High strain response to applied electrical field → piezoelectricity.
- Strong variation in polarization with temperature → pyroelectricity.

    Strong non-linear dielectric response to an applied electrical field.

Applications of Ferroelectrics

- Non-volatile RAMs
- Dynamic capacitors
- Tunable microwave devices
- Pyroelectric sensors
- Optical waveguides

All ferroelectric materials are Piezoelectric, but all Piezoelectric materials are not Ferroelectric.

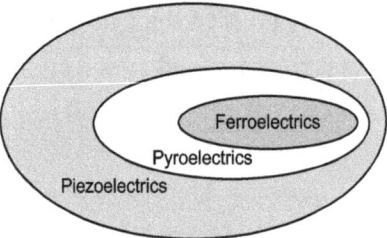

Fig. 4.8

Ferroelectrics are spontaneously polarised, but are also piezoelectric, in that their polarisation changes under the influence of a stress. This is because while all ferroelectrics are piezoelectric,but not all piezoelectrics are ferroelectric.

4.4 LOSS TANGENT

Tan δ, or Tan Delta

Tan Delta, also called Loss Angle or Dissipation Factor. tan δ testing, is a indicative method of testing cables to determine the quality of the cable insulation. This is done to predict the remaining life expectancy and in order to prioritize cable replacement. If the insulation of a cable is free from defects, such as water trees, electrical trees, moisture and air pockets, etc., the cable approaches the properties of a perfect capacitor. It is very similar to a parallel plate capacitor with the two plates separated by the insulation material. In a perfect capacitor, the voltage and current phaser are phase shifted 90 degrees and the current through the insulation is capacitive. If there are impurities in the insulation, the resistance of the insulation decreases, resulting in an increase in resistive current through the insulation. It is no longer a perfect capacitor. The current and voltage will no longer be shifted 90 degrees. It will be something less than 90 degrees. The extent to which the phase shift is less than 90 degrees is indicative of the level of insulation contagion, hence quality/reliability. This "Loss Angle" is measured and analyzed. Below is a representation of a cable. The tangent of the angle δ is measured. This will indicate the level of resistance in the insulation of cable. By measuring I_R/I_C (opposite over adjacent the tangent), we can determine the quality of the cable insulation. In a perfect cable, the angle would be nearly zero. An increasing angle indicates an increase in the resistive current through the insulation, meaning contagion. The greater the angle, the worse the cable condition.

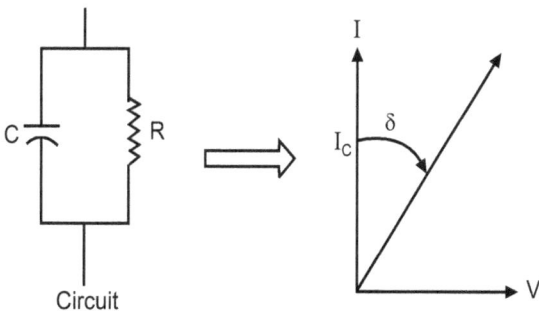

Fig. 4.9

Factors Affecting Dielectric Loss

- **Temperature** : With rise in temperature the dielectric loss also increases.
- **Moisture :** Presence of moisture in the insulating material increases the dielectric loss in the insulating material.
- **Applied Voltage :** Dielectric loss increases with rise in the applied voltage. This loss is one factor in limiting the operating voltage of underground cables generally to 100 kV.

4.5   RELATION BETWEEN D.E. & P

Consider a parallel plate capacitor having area m² for each plate and distance between it as d m. Battery voltage is V applied across it. Electric field strength is given by when there is vacuum.

$$E = \frac{V}{d} \text{ (V/m)}$$

Surface charge density is given by,

$$\sigma_0 = \frac{Q_0}{A}$$

$$= \frac{C_0 \cdot V}{A}$$

Where, Q_0 is charge.

$$\sigma_0 = \frac{\varepsilon_0 A}{d} \times \frac{V}{A}$$

$$\sigma_0 = \varepsilon_0 \frac{V}{d}$$

$$\sigma_0 = \varepsilon_0 E$$

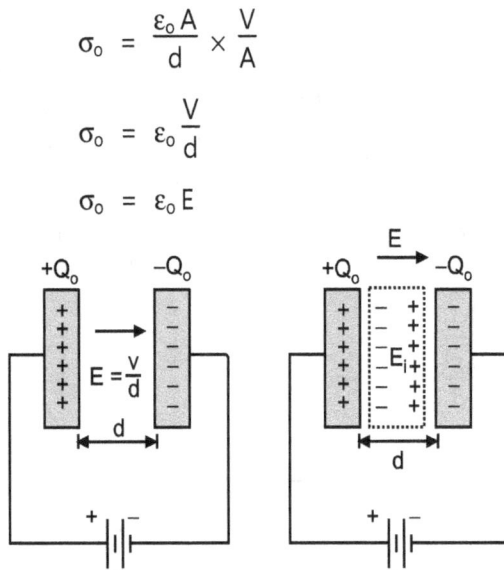

(a) When vacuum as dielectric   (b) When dielectric material is present

Fig. 4.10 : Parallel plate capacitor

Surface charge density when dielectric material is introduced between the plates of capacitor.

$$\sigma_1 = \frac{Q}{A}$$

Where, Q is charge.

$$\sigma_1 = \frac{CV}{A}$$

$$\sigma_1 = \frac{\varepsilon_0 \varepsilon_r A}{d} \frac{V}{A}$$

$$\sigma_1 = \varepsilon_0 \varepsilon_r E$$

This shows increase in charge density.

i.e. $$\sigma_1 = \sigma_0 + \sigma_P$$

Where, σ_P = Charge density due to polarization.

We know that $\qquad\qquad\qquad\sigma_p \cong P$

$\therefore \qquad\qquad\qquad\qquad\quad \sigma_p = \sigma_0 + P$

$$\varepsilon_0\, \varepsilon_r\, E = \varepsilon_0 \cdot E + P$$

$$P = \varepsilon_0\, \varepsilon_r\, E - \varepsilon_0\, E$$

$$\boxed{P = D - \varepsilon_0\, E} \qquad\qquad\qquad (\because D = \varepsilon_0\, \varepsilon_r\, E)$$

also, $\qquad\qquad\qquad\quad P = \varepsilon_r\, E\, (\varepsilon_0 - 1)$

$$P = \varepsilon_r\, E\, x_0$$

Where, x_0 is called susceptibility of dielectric material.

4.6 CLAUSIUS MOSSOTI EQUATION

Assumption in Clausius Mossotti equation.

- It is applicable to elemental solid dielectrics which only having cubic crystal structure.

- Molecule arrangement is isotropic.

- Polarizability of molecule isotropic and by elastic displacement only.

- Absence of short range interactions.

The materials like diamond, silicon exhibit only electronic polarization so for such material, $P_i = P_0 = 0$ and total polarization $P = P_e$.

$$P = N\, \alpha_e\, E_i \qquad\qquad\qquad \because (1)$$

where, α_e = electronic polarizability and E_i = internal field.

For cubic symmetry,

$$E_i = E + \frac{P}{3\varepsilon_0}$$

Putting this in equation (1),

$$P = N\, \alpha_e \left(E + \frac{P}{3\varepsilon_0} \right)$$

We know that, $\qquad\qquad P = \varepsilon_0\, (\varepsilon_r - 1)\, E$

$\therefore \qquad\qquad \varepsilon_0\, (\varepsilon_r - 1)\, E = N\, \alpha_e \left[E + \frac{E_0\, (\varepsilon_r - 1)\, E}{3\varepsilon_0} \right]$

$$\varepsilon_0 (\varepsilon_r - 1) E = N \alpha_e \left[E + \frac{(\varepsilon_r - 1) E}{3} \right]$$

$$\varepsilon_0 (\varepsilon_r - 1) E = N \alpha_e \left[1 + \frac{(\varepsilon_r - 1)}{3} \right]$$

$$\varepsilon_0 (\varepsilon_r - 1) = N \alpha_e \left[\frac{3 + (\varepsilon_r - 1)}{3} \right]$$

$$\varepsilon_0 (\varepsilon_r - 1) = N \alpha_e \frac{(\varepsilon_r - 2)}{3}$$

$$\boxed{\frac{(\varepsilon_r - 1)}{(\varepsilon_r - 2)} = \frac{N \alpha_e}{3 \varepsilon_0}}$$

SOLVED EXAMPLES

Example 4.1 : Argon gas contains 2.7×10^{25} atom at 0°C and 1 atomic pressure. Calculate dielectric constant of argon atom is 3.48 Au.

Solution :   Given : $N = 2.7 \times 10^{25}$ atoms/m^3, Diameter d = 3.48 Au = 3.48×10^{-10} m,

$$\text{Radius} = \frac{d}{2} = 1.92 \times 10^{-10} \text{ m}$$

Now, Dielectric constant,

$$\begin{aligned}
\varepsilon_r &= 1 + 4\pi N R^3 \\
&= 1 + 4 \times \pi \times 2.7 \times 10^{25} \times (1.92 \times 10^{-10})^3 \\
&= 1 + 4\pi \times 2.7 \times 10^{-5} \times (1.92)^3 \\
&= 1 + 4\pi \times 19.11 \times 10^{-5}
\end{aligned}$$

$$\boxed{\varepsilon_r = 1.0024}$$

Example 4.2 : Calculate the electronic polarizability of argon atom $\varepsilon_r = 1.0024$ and at NTP and $N = 2.7 \times 10^{25}$ atom/m^3.

Solution : Given : $\varepsilon_r = 1.0024$, $N = 2.7 \times 10^{25}$ atom/m^3

$$\begin{aligned}
\text{We know that,} \quad P &= \varepsilon_0 (\varepsilon_r - 1) E \\
P &= N \alpha_e \cdot E \\
N \alpha_e \cdot E &= \varepsilon_0 (\varepsilon_r - 1) E
\end{aligned}$$

$$\alpha_e \ =$$

$$\boxed{\alpha_e = 7.9 \times 10^{-40} \text{ Fm}^2}$$

Example 4.3 : The number of atoms in volume of one cubic meter of hydrogen gas is 9.8×10^{26}. The radius of hydrogen atom is 0.53 Au. Calculate the polarizability and relative permittivity.

Solution : **Given :** R = 0.53 Au = 0.53×10^{-10} m, N = 9.8×10^{26} atoms/m³

$$\text{Polarizability} \ = \ \alpha_e = 4\pi \, \varepsilon_0 R^3$$

$$= \ 4\pi \times 8.85 \times 10^{-12} \times (0.53 \times 10^{-10})^3$$

$$\text{Relative permittivity} \ = \ \varepsilon_r = 1 + 4\pi NR^3$$

$$= \ 1 + 4\pi \, (9.8 \times 10^{-12}) \times (0.53 \times 10^{-10})^3$$

$$\boxed{\varepsilon_r = 1.008}$$

Example 4.4 : Prove that the energy stored per unit volume in polarized atom of polarizability is $\dfrac{1}{2} \alpha \, E^2$ where E is the homogeneous field applied to the material.

Solution : In parallel plate capacitor energy stored in polarizing the dielectric is given as,

$$\omega' \ = \ \frac{1}{2} (C - C_0) \, V^2$$

$$= \ \frac{1}{2} \left(\frac{a\varepsilon_0\varepsilon_r}{d} \ - \frac{a\varepsilon_0}{d} \right) V^2 \qquad \text{... (1)}$$

where,

a = area of parallel plate.

d = distance between plates.

V = applied voltage.

we know that Polarization, is given by P = $\varepsilon_0 \, (\varepsilon_r - 1) \, E$

$$\therefore \qquad\qquad (\varepsilon_r - 1) \ = \ \frac{P}{\varepsilon_0 E}$$

From (1),

$$\omega' \ = \ \frac{1}{2} \frac{a\varepsilon_0}{d} \, (\varepsilon_r - 1) \, V^2$$

$$= \frac{1}{2} \frac{\alpha \varepsilon_0}{d} \frac{P}{\varepsilon_0 E} V^2$$

$$\omega' = \frac{1}{2} \varepsilon_0 V \left(\frac{V}{d}\right) \times a \times \frac{P}{E}$$

$$= \frac{1}{2} \varepsilon_0 \times V \times E \times \alpha \times \frac{P}{E}$$

$$\omega' = \frac{1}{2} \times V \times a \times P$$

Now, volume of dielectric $= a \times d \ m^3$

$$\frac{\omega'}{Volume} = \frac{\frac{1}{2} V a P}{ad}$$

$$= \frac{1}{2} \left(\frac{V}{d}\right) P$$

$$= \frac{1}{2} P E$$

We know that,　　　　　　　$P = \alpha E$

$$\frac{\omega'}{Volume} = \frac{1}{2} \alpha E^2$$

Hence Proved.

Example 4.5 : Two parallel plates $0.15 \times 0.30 \ m^2$ in area are separated by a dielectric of thickness 0.06 m dielectric constant $\varepsilon_r = 5.4$ the capacitor so formed is connected to a 400 V D.C. supply. Calculate

(i) The capacitance of the capacitor.

(ii) The charge on the plates of capacitor.

(iii) The electric field intensity in the dielectric.

(iv) Energy stored in condenser as well as energy stored in polarizing the dielectric.

Solution : **Given :** $a = 0.15 \times 0.30 \ m^2$, d = 0.06 m, ε = 5.4, V = 400 V.

(i) Capacitance,　　　　　$C = \dfrac{a \, \varepsilon_0 \, \varepsilon_r}{d}$

$$= \frac{(0.15 \times 0.30) \times (8.85 \times 10^{-12}) \times 5.4}{0.06}$$

$$\boxed{C = 3.585 \times 10^{-11} \ F}$$

(ii) Charge,　　　　　　　$Q = CV$

$$= 3.585 \times 10^{-11} \times 400$$

$$\boxed{Q = 1.432 \times 10^{-8} \ C}$$

(iii) Electric field intensity, $E = \dfrac{V}{d}$

$$= \dfrac{400}{0.06}$$

$$\boxed{E = 6666.67 \text{ V/m}}$$

(iv) Energy stored in condenser, $\omega = \dfrac{1}{2} CV^2$

$$= \dfrac{1}{2} \times 3.585 \times 10^{-11} \times 400^2$$

$$\boxed{\omega = 2.864 \times 10^{-6} \text{ J}}$$

We know that, $C_0 = \dfrac{C}{\varepsilon_r}$

$$= \dfrac{3.585 \times 10^{-11}}{5.4}$$

$$\boxed{C_0 = 0.6638 \times 10^{-11}}$$

Energy stored in polarizing the dielectric is,

$$\omega' = \dfrac{1}{2} (C - C_0) V^2$$

$$= \dfrac{1}{2} (3.585 - 0.6638) \times 10^{-11} \times 400^2$$

$$\boxed{\omega' = 2.336 \times 10^{-6} \text{ J}}$$

Example 4.6 : A solid contains 4×10^{28} atoms each having polarizability of 2.75×10^{-40} F/m^2. Assuming that internal field is given by Lorentz formula. Calculate the ratio of internal field to the applied electric field.

Solution : Given : $N = 4 \times 1028$; $\alpha = 2.7$/F/m^2

By using Lorentz formula the internal field is given by,

$$E_i = E + \dfrac{P}{3\varepsilon_0} \qquad\qquad \text{... (1)}$$

Polarization $P = N \alpha E_i$ $\qquad\qquad$ ... (2)

From equations (1) and (2),

$$E_i = E + \dfrac{N \alpha E_i}{3\varepsilon_0}$$

$$E = E_i - \dfrac{N \alpha E_i}{3\varepsilon_0}$$

$$E = E_i \left(1 - \dfrac{N\alpha}{3\varepsilon_0} \right)$$

$$\frac{E_i}{E} = \frac{1}{1 - \left(\dfrac{N\alpha}{3\varepsilon_0}\right)}$$

$$= \frac{1}{\left(1 - \dfrac{4 \times 10^{28} \times 2.75 \times 10^{-40}}{3 \times 8.85 \times 10^{-12}}\right)}$$

$$= \frac{1}{\left(1 - \dfrac{11 \times 10^{-12}}{26.55 \times 10^{-12}}\right)}$$

$$= \frac{1}{1 - 0.414} = \frac{1}{0.5856}$$

$$\boxed{\frac{E_i}{E} = 1.7076}$$

Example 4.7 : A solid contains 10×10^{28} atoms/m^3 each having polarizability of 1×10^{-40} Farad m^2. Assuming that the internal field is given by Lorentz formula. Find the ratio of the internal to the applied field.

Solution : Given :

$$N = 10 \times 10^{28} \text{ atom/m}^3$$
$$\alpha = 1 \times 10^{-40} \text{ Fm}^2$$

Using Lorentz formula internal field is given by,

$$E_i = E + \frac{P}{3\varepsilon_0}$$

where,

$$P = N\alpha E_i$$

$$E_i = E + \frac{N\alpha E_i}{3\varepsilon_0}$$

$$E_i\left(1 - \frac{N\alpha}{3\varepsilon_0}\right) = E$$

$$\frac{E_i}{E} = \frac{1}{\left(1 - \dfrac{N\alpha}{3\varepsilon_0}\right)}$$

$$= \frac{1}{\left(1 - \dfrac{10 \times 10^{28} \times 1 \times 10^{-40}}{3 \times 8.85 \times 10^{-12}}\right)}$$

$$= \frac{1}{\left(1 - \dfrac{10 \times 10^{-12}}{26.55 \times 10^{-12}}\right)}$$

$$\boxed{\frac{E_i}{E} = 1.6042}$$

Example 4.8 : When sodium chloride crystal is subjected to an electric field of 1000 V/m, the resultant polarization is 4.3×10^{-8} C/m^2. Calculate the relative permittivity of sodium chloride crystal.

Solution : Given :

$$E = 1000 \text{ V/m}$$

$$\alpha = 4.3 \times 10^{-8} \text{ c/m}^2$$

Polarization, $P = \varepsilon_0 (\varepsilon_r - 1) E$

$$(\varepsilon_r - 1) = \frac{P}{\varepsilon_0 E}$$

$$\varepsilon_r = 1 + \frac{P}{\varepsilon_0 E}$$

$$= 1 + \frac{4.3 \times 10^{-8}}{8.85 \times 10^{-12} \times 1000}$$

$$\boxed{\varepsilon_r = 5.86}$$

Example 4.9 : A solid contains 7×10^{26} identical atoms/m^2 each with polarizability of 2×10^{-38} farad m^2. Assuming that internal field is given by Lorentz formula. Calculate the ratio of internal field to the applied field.

Solution : Given :

$$E = 7 \times 10^{26} \text{ atoms/m}^2$$

$$\alpha = 2 \times 10^{-38} \text{ Fm}^2$$

The internal field using Lorentz formula is given by,

$$E_i = E + \frac{P}{3\varepsilon_0}$$

where, $P = N \alpha E_i$

$$E_i = E + \frac{N \alpha E_i}{3\varepsilon_0}$$

$$E_i \left(1 - \frac{N\alpha}{3\varepsilon_0} \right) = E$$

$$\frac{E_i}{E} = \frac{1}{\left(1 - \dfrac{N\alpha}{3\varepsilon_0} \right)}$$

$$= \frac{1}{\left(1 - \dfrac{7 \times 10^{26} \times 2 \times 10^{-38}}{3 \times 8.85 \times 10^{-12}} \right)}$$

$$\boxed{\frac{E_i}{E} = 2.1155}$$

Example 4.10 : A parallel plate has capacitance of 5 μF. The dielectric has permittivity $\varepsilon_r = 100$; for an applied voltage of 2000 V. Find energy stored in capacitor as well as energy stored in polarizing the dielectric.

Solution : Given :

$$C = 5\,\mu F$$

$$\varepsilon_r = 100$$

$$V = 2000\ V$$

Energy stored in capacitor,

$$\omega = \frac{1}{2}CV^2$$

$$= \frac{1}{2} \times 5 \times 10^{-6} \times (2000)^2$$

$$\boxed{\omega = 10\ J}$$

$$C_o = \frac{C}{\varepsilon_r}$$

$$= \frac{5}{100}\ \mu F$$

$$\boxed{C_o = 0.05 \times 10^{-6}\ F}$$

Energy stored in polarizing the dielectric,

$$\omega' = \frac{1}{2}(C - C_o) \cdot V^2$$

$$= \frac{1}{2}(5 - 0.05) \times 10^{-6} \times (2000)^2$$

$$\boxed{\omega' = 9.9\ J}$$

Example 4.11 : A solid contains 6×10^{28} atom each having polarizability of 2.85×10^{-40} F m^2. Assuming that internal field is given by Lorentz formula. Calculate ratio of internal field to the applied electric field.

Solution : Given :

$$N = 6 \times 10^{28}\ atom$$

$$\alpha = 2.85 \times 10^{-40}\ Fm^2$$

We know that,

$$E_i = E + \frac{P}{3\varepsilon_o}$$

Polarization, $$P = N\,\alpha\,E_i$$

$$E_i = E + \frac{N\,\alpha\,E_i}{3\varepsilon_o}$$

$$\frac{E_i}{E} = \frac{1}{1 - \dfrac{N\alpha}{3\varepsilon_o}}$$

$$= \frac{1}{\left(1 - \dfrac{6 \times 10^{28} \times 2.85 \times 10^{-40}}{3 \times 8.85 \times 10^{-12}}\right)}$$

$$\boxed{\frac{E_i}{E} = 2.8095}$$

Example 4.12 : If sodium chloride crystal is subjected to an electric field of 2000 V/m the resultant polarization is 4.3×10^{-8} C/m². Calculate the relative permittivity of sodium chloride crystal.

Solution : Given :

$$P = 4.3 \times 10^{-8} \text{ C/m}^2$$

$$E = 2000 \text{ V/m}$$

Polarization,

$$P = \varepsilon_o (\varepsilon_r - 1) E$$

$$(\varepsilon_r - 1) = \frac{P}{\varepsilon_o E}$$

$$\varepsilon_r = 1 + \frac{P}{\varepsilon_o E}$$

$$\varepsilon_r = 1 + \frac{4.3 \times 10^{-8}}{(8.85 \times 10^{-12}) \times 2000}$$

$$\boxed{\varepsilon_r = 3.429}$$

Example 4.13 : The number of atoms in volume of one cubic meter of hydrogen gas is 9.8×10^{26}. The radius of hydrogen atom is 0.53 Au. Calculate the polarizability and relative permittivity.

Solution : Given :

$$N = 9.8 \times 10^{26}, T = 0.53 \text{ Au}$$

Polarizability

$$2e = 4\pi\varepsilon_o R^3$$

$$= 4 \times \pi \times 8.85 \times 10^{-12} \times (0.53 \times 10^{-10})^3$$

$$\boxed{2e = 1.66 \times 10^{-41} \text{ Fm}^2}$$

Relative permittivity $= 1 + 4\pi N R^3$

$$= 1 + 4\pi \times (9.8 \times 10^{-12}) \times (0.53 \times 10^{-10})^3$$

$$\boxed{\varepsilon_r = 1.008}$$

Example 4.14 : If sodium chloride crystal is subjected to an electric field of 2000 V/m and the resultant polarization is 4.8×10^{-8} C/m^2. Calculate the relative permittivity of sodium chloride.

Solution : **Given :** E = 2000 V/m, P = 4.8×10^{-8}C/me

We know that P $= \varepsilon_o (\varepsilon_r - 1)$ E

$$\frac{P}{\varepsilon_o E} = \varepsilon_r - 1$$

$$\varepsilon_r = 1 + \frac{P}{\varepsilon_o E}$$

$$\varepsilon_r = 1 + \frac{4.8 \times 10^{-8}}{8.85 \times 10^{-12} \times 2000}$$

$$\boxed{\varepsilon_r = 3.71}$$

Example 4.15 : A parallel plate has capacitance of 5 µF. The dielectric has permittivity $\varepsilon_r = 100$ for an applied voltage of 1000 V. Find (i) Energy stored in the capacitor (ii) The energy stored in polarizing electric.

Solution : **Given :** $\varepsilon_r = 100$, V = 1000 V, C 5 = µF.

Energy stored in capacitor is given as,

$$\omega = \frac{1}{2} CV^2$$

$$= \frac{1}{2} \times 5 \times 10^{-6} \times 1000^2$$

$$\boxed{\omega = 2.5 \text{ J}}$$

$$C_o = \frac{C}{\varepsilon_r}$$

$$= \frac{5}{100} \times 10^{-6}$$

$$\boxed{C_o = 0.05 \times 10^{-6} \text{ F}}$$

Energy stored in polarizing the dielectric,

$$\omega' = \frac{1}{2} (C - C_o) V^2$$

$$= \frac{1}{2} (5 - 0.05) \times 10^{-6} \times 1000^2$$

$$\boxed{\omega' = 2.475 \text{ J}}$$

Example 4.16 : A slid contains 4×10^{28} atoms each having polarizability of 2.75×10^{-40} F/m^2. Assuming that internal field is given by Lorentz formula. Calculate the ratio of internal field to the applied field.

Solution :   Given : N = 4×10^{28} atoms., $\alpha = 2.75 \times 10^{-40}$ F/m^2.

We know that,

$$E_i = E + \frac{P}{3\varepsilon_o}$$

Where,

$$P = N \alpha E_i$$

$\therefore$

$$E_i = E + \frac{N \alpha E_i}{3\varepsilon_o}$$

$$E_i \left(1 - \frac{N\alpha}{3\varepsilon_o}\right) = E$$

$$\frac{E_i}{E} = \frac{1}{\left(1 - \dfrac{N\alpha}{3\varepsilon_o}\right)} = \frac{1}{1 - \dfrac{4 \times 10^{28} \times 2.75 \times 10^{-40}}{3 \times 8.85 \times 10^{-12}}}$$

$$\boxed{\frac{E_i}{E} = 1.70}$$

Example 4.17 : Calculate the electronic polarizability of argon atom if ε_r = 1.0024 at NTP and N = 2.8×10^{25} atom/m^2.

Solution :   Given : ε_e = 1.0023, N = 2.8×10^{25} atom/m^2

We know that,

$$P = \varepsilon_o (\varepsilon_r - 1) E$$

also,

$$P = N \alpha_e E$$

$$N \alpha_e E = \varepsilon_o (\varepsilon_r - 1) E$$

$$\alpha_o = \frac{\varepsilon_o (\varepsilon_r - 1)}{N}$$

$$= \frac{8.85 \times 10^{-12} (1.0024 - 1)}{2.8 \times 10^{25}}$$

$$\alpha_e = 0.007585 \times 10^{-37}$$

$$\boxed{\alpha_e = 7.58 \times 10^{-40} \text{ Fm}^2}$$

QUESTIONS

1. Prove that $\rho = \varepsilon_0(\varepsilon_r - 1)E$

2. Define and explain

   (i)   Piezoelectricity   (ii) Ferroelectricity

   (iii)   Relative permittivity   (iv) Dielectric loss and loss tangent

   (v)   Polarization

3. Explain different types of polarization.

4. Explain construction of photo emissive cell.

5. Explain photo conductive cell.

6. Explain PV module.

7. Explain loss tangent and its significance.

8. Write note on piezo electricity.

9. Explain term polarization of dielectric. Explain electronic polarization and orientation polarization.

10. Define

    (i) Electric Dipole moment   (ii) Dielectric constant

    (iii) Electric flux density   (iv) Polarizability

11. Derive Clausius Mosotti equation from the first principle applied to dielectric materials. Give Debye's generalization of this relation stating the assumptions to make to draw the relation.

12. Explain

    (i) Ferro electricity   (ii) Loss tangent and its significance

13. What is meant by loss tangent as referred to polar directions. Hence give this significance.

14. Define

    (i) Electric dipole moment   (ii) Dielectric constant

    (iii) Polarizability   (iv) Pyro electricity

15. Derive Clausius Mosotti equation from the first principle applied to dielectric materials stating the assumptions made to draw the relation.

16. Derive Clausius Mosotti equation from the first principle applied to dielectric materials stating the assumptions made to draw the relation.

17. Write a note on piezoelectricity.

18. Drive Clausius Mossotti relation from first principle applied to dielectric materials stating the assumptions made to draw the relation.

19. Explain the following

    (a) Loss tangent and its significance (b) Ferro-electricity

    (c) Piezo-electricity

14. If sodium chloride crystal is subjected to an electric field of 2000 V/m and the resultant polarization is 4.8×10^{-8} c/m^2. Calculate the relative permittivity of sodium chloride.

16. Describe the polarization process in detail. Why and how does it occurs?

17. Explain ionic polarization in detail. How is it different from oriental polarization?

18. Explain the term polarisation. With neat diagram explain electronic polarisation.

19. Explain the following terms

    (i) Loss tangent   (ii) Ferro-electricity

20. A parallel plate has capacitance of 5 μF. The dielectric has permittivity ε_r = 100, for an applied voltage of 1000 V.

    Find

    (i) Energy stored in the capacitor (ii) The energy stored in polarising the dielectric

21. A solid contains 4×10^{28} atoms each having polarizability of 2.75×10^{-40} F/m^2. Assuming that internal field is given by Lorentz formula. Calculate the ratio of internal field to the applied field.

22. Calculate the electronic polarizability of argon atom if ε_r = 1.0024 at NTP and N = 2.8 $\times$ 10^{25} atoms per m^3.

23. Derive Clausius-Mosotti relation from the first principle applied to dielectric materials. State the assumptions.

24. What is meant by loss tangent as referred to polar dielectrics? Give its significance.

25. Explain the following

    (i) Ferro-electricity

    (ii) Electronic polarization

26. Calculate the electronic polarizability of ARgon atom. Given ε_r = 1.0024 at NTP and $N = 2.8 \times 10^{25}$ atoms/m³.

27. Explain orientation polarization in detail. How is it different than ionic polarization?

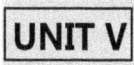

PRINCIPLES OF ELECTRO-MECHANICAL ENERGY CONVERSION

5.1 INTRODUCTION

Electromechanical devices are developed for energy conversion between electrical and mechanical forms. Electromechanical energy conversion devices can be divided into following three categories:

(1) Transducers : These devices transform the signals of different forms. Examples are microphones, pickups, and speakers.

(2) Force Producing Devices : These type of devices produce forces mostly for linear motion drives, such as relays, solenoids (linear actuators), and electromagnets.

(3) Continuous Energy Conversion Equipment : These devices operate in rotating mode.

A device would be known as a generator if it convert mechanical energy into electrical energy, or as a motor if it converts from electrical to mechanical.

Permeability of ferromagnetic materials is much larger than the permittivity of dielectric materials, it is more advantageous to use electromagnetic field as the medium for electromechanical energy conversion.

Fig. 5.1 below shows an electromechanical system . It consists of

- **Electrical Subsystem :** Electric circuits such as windings
- **Magnetic Subsystem :** Magnetic field in the magnetic cores and airgaps
- **Mechanical Subsystem :** Mechanically movable parts such as a plunger in a linear actuator and a rotor in a rotating electrical machine
- **Voltages and Currents :** It is used to describe the state of the electrical subsystem and they are governed by the basic circuital laws OHM's law, KCL and KVL.
- **Mechanical Subsystem :** It can be described in terms of positions, velocities, and accelerations, and is governed by the Newton's laws.
- **The Field Quantities :** Magnetic flux, flux density, and field strength, are governed by the Maxwell's equations.
- When coupled with an electric circuit, the magnetic flux interacting with the current in the circuit would produce a force or torque on a mechanically movable part.

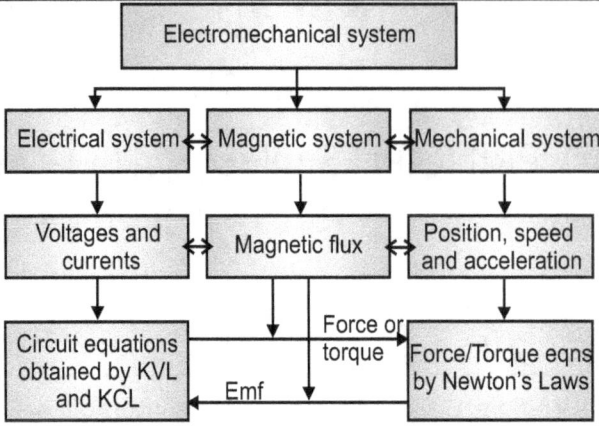

Fig. 5.1 : Electromechanical system modeling

5.2   FORCE AND TORQUE IN ELECTRIC MACHINES

In electric motors the electric energy is converted into mechanical energy. In electric generator a mechanical energy is converted into electrical energy. In both cases the magnetic field is the medium in the electromechanical conversion process.

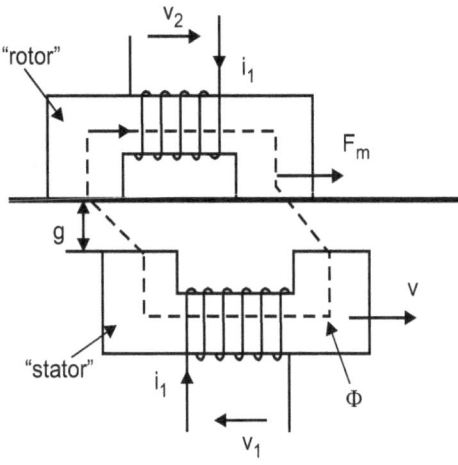

Fig. 5.2

In the linear synchronous motor the electric energy is delivered to the system through the "stator" and "rotor" winding terminals called electrical ports. This energy is converted to the energy of magnetic field, which is next converted into mechanical energy. This process of energy conversion is shown schematically in Fig. 5.3.

For the generator the process is the mechanical energy is delivered to the rotor through a rotor shaft and due to the magnetic flux generated by the rotor current it is converted into electrical energy leaving the system through the stator winding terminals

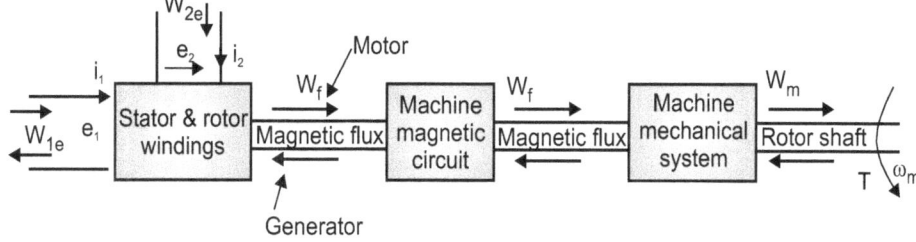

Fig. 5.3 : Diagram of electromechanical energy conversion

In the rotor and stator windings a part of electrical energy is converted into heat due to Ohmic power losses in the winding resistance. In the rotor and stator cores, part of field energy is lost. In the mechanical part of the system part of mechanical energy is lost as heat in bearings and due to the friction and windage losses. The process of energy conversion with inclusion of power losses is shown in Fig. 5.4. These power losses are converted into the heat energy.

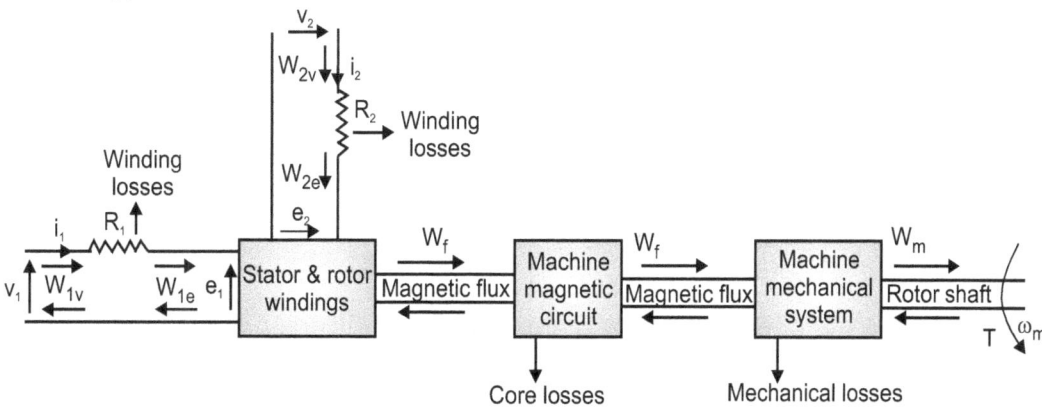

Fig. 5.4 : Diagram of electromechanical energy conversion with power losses

5.3 ENERGY IN MAGNETIC SYSTEMS

Field energy In motor and generator ;the field energy is converted either into electric or mechanical energy. In permanent magnet machine the magnetic flux is generated by the magnet and in case of electromagnet the magnetic field is generated by the current. Let us consider the electromagnetic structure shown in Fig. 5.5 to determine the magnetic field energy stored in the motor. It consist of primary part, which is stationary and the secondary part, that can move and which does not have the winding. If we increase now the current in the primary winding from 0 to i1. The magnetic flux will rise from 0 to $\Phi 1$ as shown in Fig. 5.6. Magnetic flux is the product of a number of winding turns and the magnetic flux

$$\lambda = N \cdot \Phi$$

In magnetic circuit the λ-i curve is not linear due to the saturation of the iron core. For the linear magnetic circuit the λ-i characteristic is a straight line as shown in Fig. 5.6 (b).

$$\lambda = L \cdot i$$

where

L is a current i coefficient known as winding inductance.

differentiate both sides of the above equation

Let L = const,

The equation for the voltage e induced in the winding

$$e = \frac{d\lambda}{dt} = L\frac{di}{dt}$$

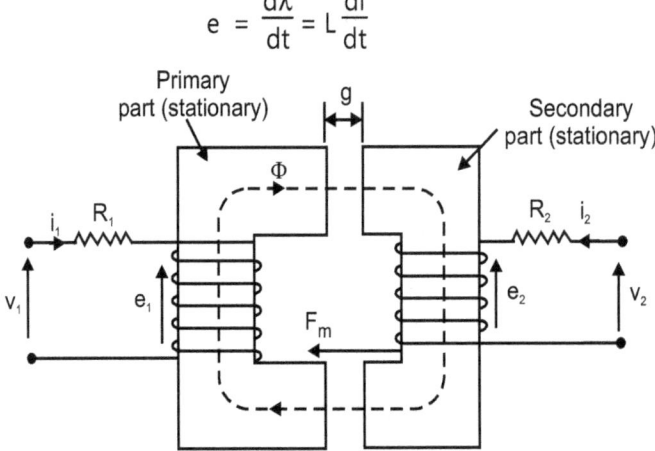

Fig. 5.5 : Illustration to derivation of formula for field energy

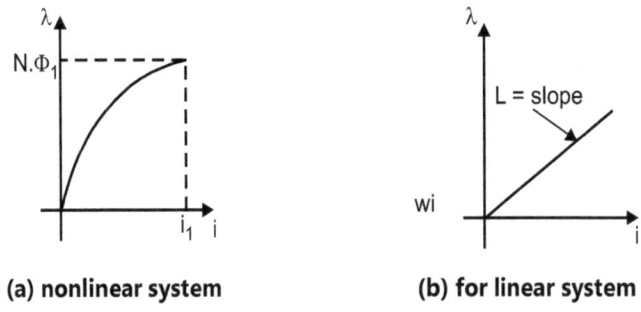

(a) nonlinear system   (b) for linear system

Fig. 5.6 : Magnetic linkage-current characteristic for

The electric power is equal

$$P_e = e \cdot i = L\frac{di}{dt}\, i$$

Relation between the power and energy is

$$\frac{dW_e}{dt} = P_e$$

The increment of electric energy

$$dW_e = P_e \cdot dt = e \cdot i \cdot dt = L \cdot i \cdot di$$

Energy is a part of the total electric energy delivered to the winding

$$dW_v = P_v \cdot dt$$
$$P_v = v \cdot i = R \cdot i^2 + e \cdot i$$

We is equal to the magnetic field energy stored in the magnetic flux:

$$W_e = W_f$$

If the power losses in all elements of the system are ignored and the secondary part is moving, then, during the differential time interval dt the increment of electrical energy dW_e is equal to the sum:

$$dW_e = dW_f + dW_m$$

where

dW_m is the increment of mechanical energy equal to mechanical work done during the time dt by the moving secondary part.

When the flux linkage is increased from zero to λ1 by means of increase of current from 0 to i1, the energy stored in the field is

$$W_f = \int_0^{\lambda_1} i\, d\lambda$$

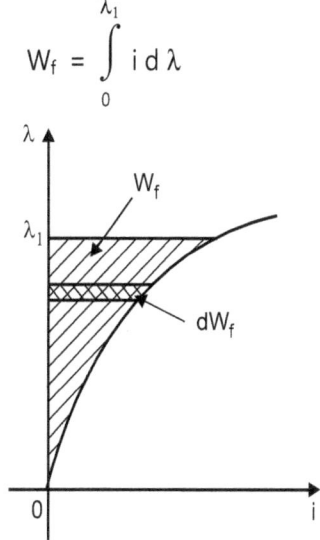

Fig. 5.7 : Field energy on λ-i characteristic

Suppose the air gap of the system increases. The λ-i characteristic will become more flat and straight as shown in Fig. 5.8. To maintain the same magnetic flux greater current should flow in the winding and consequently greater energy is stored in the magnetic circuit . Since the volume of magnetic core remained unchanged the increase of field energy occurred in the air-gap.

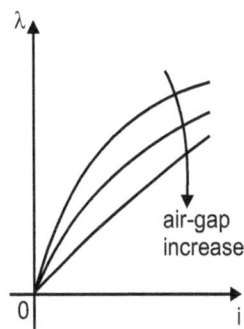

Fig. 5.8 : λ-I characteristics for various air-gaps in the machine

Fig. 5.9 : Field energy in the machine with different air-gap

The energy stored in the field can be expressed in terms of magnetic flux density B in the air gap g. To find flux density B for a given current i in the winding consider the equivalent magnetic circuit of the system shown in Fig. 5.10. Analogy between the electric and magnetic quantities are shown in Table 5.1.

Table 5.1

Electric Circuit	Magnetic Circuit
Electromotive force (emf) E [V] Current I [A]	Magnetomotive (mmf) $F_m = I \cdot N$ [A turns] Magnetic flux Φ [Wb]
Resistance of conductor $$R = \frac{l_w}{A_w \gamma} \ [\Omega]$$ where l_w – length of wire [m] A_w – cross-section area of the wire (m^2) γ – conductivity Ohm's law $$i = \frac{E}{R}$$	Magnetic resistance (reluctance) of magnetic circuit $$Rm = \frac{l_m}{A_m \mu} \ [1/H]$$ where l_m – length of magnetic circuit [m], A_m – cross-section are of magnetic circuit [m^2] μ – magnetic permeability [H/m] $$\Phi = \frac{F_m}{R_m}$$

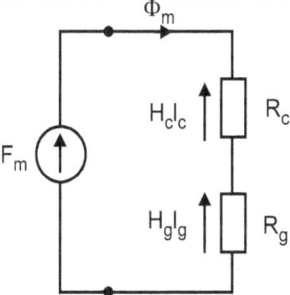

Fig. 5.10 : Equivalent magnetic circuit of the electromagnetic system

Magnetic flux Φ is a product of B [T] $\rightarrow$ magnetic flux density, and Am [m^2]

$$\Phi = B \cdot A_m$$

For the linear magnetic circuit a flux density is equal

$$B = H \cdot \mu$$

where H $\rightarrow$ is the magnetic field intensity in the magnetic circuit.

Ohm's law for magnetic circuit is:

$$F_m = \Phi \cdot R_m$$

$$I \cdot N = B \cdot A_m \frac{l_m}{A_m \mu}$$

$$= H \cdot \mu \frac{l_m}{\mu}$$

$$= H \cdot l_m$$

where H·lm is the magnetic voltage drop across reluctance of the magnetic circuit.

Consider now the electromagnetic system with its magnetic equivalent circuit in Fig. 5.10. Let

Hc $\rightarrow$ magnetic intensity in the core

Hg $\rightarrow$ magnetic intensity in the air gap

lc $\rightarrow$ total length of the magnetic core

lg $\rightarrow$ length of the air-gaps

Then

$$N \cdot i_1 = H_c l_c + H_g l_g$$

$$\lambda = N \cdot \Phi = N \cdot A_m \cdot B$$

The flux linkage For the air-gap

$$W_f = \int \frac{H_c l_c + H_g l_g}{N} N \cdot A_m \cdot dl$$

$$H_g = \frac{B}{\mu_0}$$

where, $\mu_0 \rightarrow$ is the magnetic permeability of the vacuum (air-gap) = $4\pi \times 10^{-7}$ [H/m]

For a linear magnetic core:

$$H_c = \frac{B_c}{\mu_c}$$

$$W_{fc} = \int \frac{B_c}{\mu_c} dB_c \cdot V_c = \frac{B_c^2}{2\mu_c} \cdot V_c$$

the field energy is inversely proportional to the permeability μ and straight proportional to the volume V. If we have the electromechanical system in which the same flux density is in both iron cores and air-gap, the magnetic energy is stored mainly in the air-gap, since the core permeability is equal to

$$\mu_c = \mu_0 \mu_r$$

5.4 CO-ENERGY

It is defined as $$W'_f = \int_0^{t_1} \lambda \cdot di$$

It does not have any physical significance. Co-energy and energy of the system is shown in Fig. 5.11.

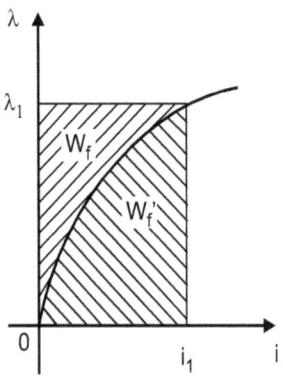

Fig. 5.11 : Field energy W$_f$ and field co-energy

$$W'_f + W_f = \lambda \cdot i$$

If λ-i characteristic is nonlinear

$$W'_f > W_f$$

but if λ-i characteristic is linear

$$W'_f = W_f$$

If the air-gap increases from g_1 to g_2 and the current remains unchanged the co-energy will decrease as shown in Fig. 5.12

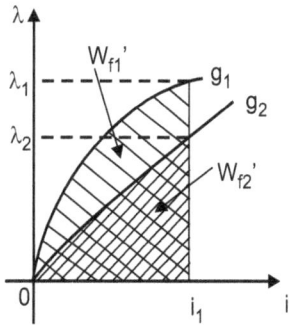

Fig. 5.12 : Field co-energy for two different values of air-gap in the system

5.5   SINGLY EXCITED SYSTEM

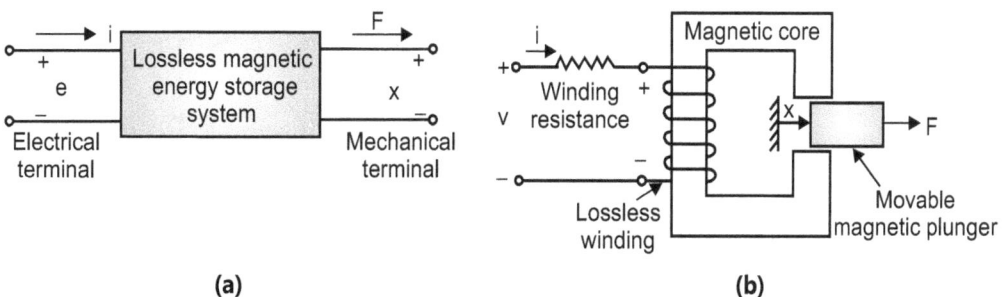

(a)   (b)

Fig. 5.13 : Single excited system

Consider a singly excited linear actuator as shown in Fig. 5.13.

winding resistance = R. At a certain time instant t,

terminal voltage applied to the excitation winding = v,

excitation winding current =i,

position of the movable plunger =x,

force acting on the plunger = F

After a time interval dt, consider that the plunger has moved for a distance dx under the action of the force F.

The mechanical done by the force acting on the plunger during this time interval is

$$dW_m = fdx$$

The amount of electrical energy that has been transferred into the magnetic field and converted into the mechanical work during this time interval can be calculated by subtracting the power loss dissipated in the winding resistance from the total power fed into the excitation winding as,

$$dW_e = dW_f + dW_m = vidt - Ri^2 dt$$

$$e = \frac{d\lambda}{dt} = v - Ri$$

$$dW_f = dW_e - dW_m = e_i d_t - Fdx$$

$$= id\lambda - Fdx$$

Energy stored in the magnetic field is a function of the flux linkage of the excitation winding and the position of the plunger.

Mathematically,

$$dW_f(\lambda, x) = \frac{dW_f(\lambda, x)}{\partial\lambda} d\lambda + \frac{\partial W_f(\lambda, x)}{\partial x} dx$$

comparing the above two equations, we get,

$$i = \frac{\partial W_f(\lambda, x)}{\partial\lambda} \text{ and } F = -\frac{\partial W_f(\lambda, x)}{\partial\lambda}$$

Energy stored in a magnetic field can be expressed as,

$$W_f(\lambda, x) = \int_0^\lambda i(\lambda, x) \, d\lambda$$

For a magnetically linear system, the above expression becomes,

$$W_f(\lambda, x) = \frac{1}{2}\frac{\lambda^2}{L(x)}$$

and the force acting on the plunger is then

$$F = -\frac{\partial W_f(\lambda, x)}{\partial x} = \frac{1}{2}\left[\frac{\lambda}{L(x)}\right]^2 \frac{dL(x)}{dx} = \frac{1}{2}i^2\frac{dL(x)}{dx}$$

In the Fig. 5.14, it is seen that the magnetic energy is equivalent to the area above the magnetization curve.

Mathematically, the area underneath the magnetization curve as the coenergy i.e.

$$W'_f(i, x) = i\lambda - W_f(\lambda, x)$$

We can obtain

$$dW'_f(i, x) = \lambda di + id\lambda - dW_f(\lambda, x)$$

$$= \lambda di + Fdx$$

$$= \frac{\partial W'_f(i, x)}{\partial i} di + \frac{\partial W'_f(i, x)}{\partial x} dx$$

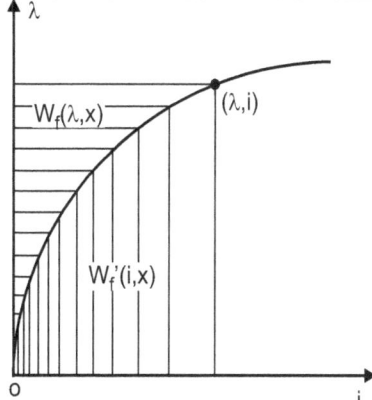

Fig. 5.14 : Energy and coenergy

$$\lambda = \frac{\partial W'_f (i, x)}{\partial i} \quad \text{and} \quad F = \frac{\partial W'_f (i, x)}{\partial x}$$

From the above diagram, the coenergy or the area underneath the magnetization curve can be calculated by

$$W'_f (i, x) = \int_0^t \lambda (i, x) \, di$$

For a magnetically linear system, the above expression becomes

$$W'_f (i, x) = \frac{1}{2} i^2 L (x)$$

the force acting on the plunger is then

$$F = \frac{\partial W'_f (i, x)}{\partial x} = \frac{1}{2} i^2 \frac{dL(x)}{dx}$$

5.6　SINGLY EXCITED ROTATING SYSTEM

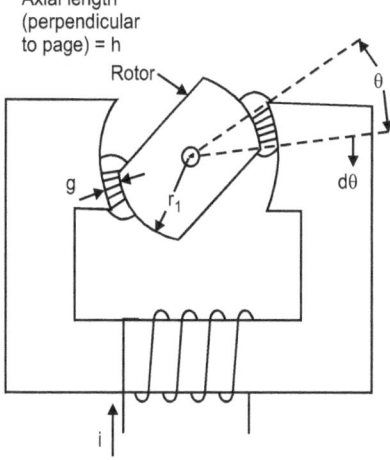

Fig. 5.15 : Singly excited rotating system

The singly excited linear system becomes a singly excited rotating system if the linearly movable plunger is replaced by a rotor. Through a derivation similar to that for a singly excited linear system, one can readily obtain that the torque acting on the rotor can be expressed as the negative partial derivative of the energy stored in the magnetic field against the angular displacement or as the positive partial derivative of the coenergy against the angular displacement, as summarized in the following table 5.2.

Table 5.2 : Torque in a singly excited rotating acuator

Energy	Coenergy
In general, $$dW_f = id\lambda - Td\theta$$ $$W_f(\lambda, \theta) = \int_0^\lambda i(\lambda, \theta)\, d\lambda$$ $$i = \frac{\partial W_f(\lambda, \theta)}{\partial \lambda}$$ $$T = -\frac{\partial W_f(\lambda, \theta)}{\partial \theta}$$	In general, $$dW'_f = \lambda di + Td\theta$$ $$W'_f(i, \theta) = \int_0^i \lambda(i, \theta)\, di$$ $$\lambda = \frac{\partial W'_f(i, \theta)}{\partial i}$$ $$T = \frac{\partial W'_f(i, \theta)}{\partial \theta}$$
If the permeability is a constant $$W_f(\lambda, \theta) = \frac{1}{2}\frac{\lambda^2}{L(\theta)}$$ $$T = \frac{1}{2}\left[\frac{\lambda}{L(\theta)}\right]^2 \frac{dL(\theta)}{d\theta} = \frac{1}{2}i^2\frac{dL(\theta)}{d\theta}$$	$$W'_f(i, \theta) = \frac{1}{2}i^2 L(\theta)$$ $$T = \frac{1}{2}i^2\frac{dL(\theta)}{d\theta}$$

5.7 DOUBLY EXCITED ROTATING SYSTEM

The general principle for force and torque calculation discussed above is equally applicable to multi-excited systems. Consider a doubly excited rotating system shown in the Fig. 5.16. The differential energy and coenergy functions can be derived as following

$$dW_e \qquad = e_1 i_1 dt + e_2 i_2 dt$$

$$e_1 = \frac{d\lambda_1}{dt}, e_2 = \frac{d\lambda_2}{dt}$$

$$dW_m = Td\theta$$

$$dW_f(\lambda_1, \lambda_2, \theta) = i_1 d\lambda_1 + i_2 d\lambda_2 - Td\theta$$

$$= \frac{\partial W_f(\lambda_1, \lambda_2, \theta)}{\partial \lambda_1}d\lambda_1 + \frac{\partial W_f(\lambda_1, \lambda_2, \theta)}{\partial \lambda_2}d\lambda_2 + \frac{\partial W_f(\lambda_1, \lambda_2, \theta)}{\partial \theta}d\theta$$

$$dW'_f (i_1, i_2, \theta) = d [i_1\lambda_1 + i_2\lambda_2 - W_f (\lambda_1, \lambda_2, \theta)$$

$$= \lambda_1 di_1 + \lambda_2 di_2 + T d\theta$$

$$= \frac{\partial W'_f (i_1, i_2, \theta)}{\partial i_1} di_1 + \frac{\partial W'_f (i_2, i_2, \theta)}{\partial i_2} di_2$$

$$+ \frac{\partial W'_f (i_1, i_2, \theta)}{\partial \theta} d\theta$$

$$T = -\frac{\partial W_f (\lambda_1, \lambda_2, \theta)}{\partial \theta}$$

$$T = -\frac{\partial W_f (i_1, i_2, \theta)}{\partial \theta}$$

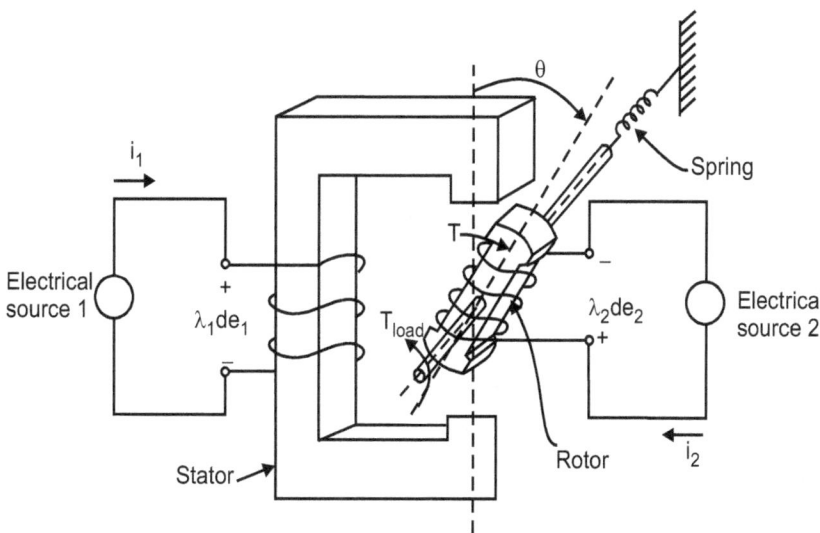

Fig. 5.16 : A doubly excited actuator

$$dW_f = dW_e - dW_m$$

For magnetically linear systems, currents and flux linkages can be related by constant inductances as following

$$\begin{bmatrix} \lambda_1 \\ \lambda_2 \end{bmatrix} = \begin{bmatrix} L_{11} & L_{12} \\ L_{21} & L_{22} \end{bmatrix} \begin{bmatrix} i_1 \\ i_2 \end{bmatrix}$$

$$\begin{bmatrix} i_1 \\ i_2 \end{bmatrix} = \begin{bmatrix} \Gamma_{11} & \Gamma_{12} \\ \Gamma_{21} & \Gamma_{22} \end{bmatrix} \begin{bmatrix} \lambda_1 \\ \lambda_2 \end{bmatrix}$$

Where

$$L_{12} = L_{21} , \Gamma_{11} = \frac{L_{22}}{\Delta}, \quad \Gamma_{12} = \Gamma_{21} = -\frac{L_{12}}{\Delta}, \quad \Gamma_{22} = \frac{L_{11}}{\Delta} \text{ and } \Delta = L_{11} L_{22} - L_{12}^2$$

The magnetic energy and coenergy can then be expressed as

$$W_f(\lambda_1, \lambda_2, \theta) = \frac{1}{2}\Gamma_{11}\lambda_1^2 + \frac{1}{2}\Gamma_{22}\lambda_2^2 + \Gamma_{12}\lambda_1\lambda_2$$

$$W'_f(i_1, i_2, \theta) = \frac{1}{2}L_{11}i_1^2 + \frac{1}{2}L_{22}i_2^2 + L_{12}i_1i_2$$

respectively, it can be shown that they are equal.

Therefore, the torque acting on the rotor can be calculated as

$$T = -\frac{\partial W_f(\lambda_1, \lambda_2, \theta)}{\partial\theta} = \frac{\partial W'_f(i_1, i_2, \theta)}{\partial\theta}$$

$$= \frac{1}{2}i_1^2\frac{dL_{11}(\theta)}{\partial\theta} + \frac{1}{2}i_2^2\frac{dL_{22}(\theta)}{\partial\theta} + i_1i_2\frac{dL_{12}(\theta)}{d\theta}$$

Because of the salient structure of the rotor, the self inductance of the stator is a function of the rotor position.

QUESTIONS

1. What are the Electromechanical systems ?
2. Explain the force and torque in Electromechanical Energy conversion.
3. Draw and explain the diagram of Electromechanical energy conversion.
4. Explain the energy in magnetic systems.
5. Derive the derivation of formula for field energy.
6. Draw and derive the field energy on λ-i characteristics.
7. Derive to co-energy system.
8. Explain and neat diagram of field energy in the machine with different air-gap.
9. Explain the singly excited system.
10. Derive and draw the magnetization curve as the co-energy.
11. Explain the singly rotating system.
12. Write a different torque in a singly excited rotating actuator.
13. Explain the doubly excited rotating system.
14. Derive the expression of doubly excited rotating system.

✠ ✠ ✠

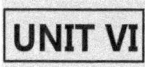

MATERIALS FOR DIRECT ENERGY CONVERSION DEVICES

6.1 THERMIONIC CONVERTER

In 1873, the Britain professor Frederic Guthrie invented the Thermionic phenomenon. In 1883, Thomas A. Edison observed that the electrons are emitted from a metal surface when it was heated. This effect is called Edison effect. After Fleming, Owen Willans Richardson worked with thermionic emission and received a Nobel Prize in 1928 "for his work on the thermionic phenomenon and especially for the discovery of the law named after him.

A thermionic energy converter (or) thermionic power generator is a device which consists of two electrodes placed near one another in a vacuum. One electrode is normally called the cathode, or emitter and the other is called the anode, or plate. Electrons in the cathode are prevented from escaping from the surface by a potential energy barrier. When an electron starts to move away from the surface, it induces a corresponding positive charge in the material, which tends to pull it back into the surface. The electron must acquire enough energy to overcome this energy barrier. At ordinary temperatures, electrons cannot acquire enough energy to escape. When the cathode is very hot, the electron energies are greatly increased by thermal motion. At sufficiently high temperatures, a considerable number of electrons are able to escape. The liberation of electrons from a hot surface is called thermionic emission. Fig. 6.1 shows thermionic converter.

- **Thermionic Effect :** Thermionic effect is the ejection of electron from the heated metal surface and forms as electron cloud at the cathode. The number of electron emitted from the metal surface depends on temperature and work function (φ). Work Function (φ): For Electrons to leave the surface of the metal, they have to be supplied with enough Energy. This minimum energy required to allow an electron to be liberated from a material as its work function (φ). Work Function differs from material to material.

- **Law of Richardson**

Richardson law states that the emission current density is exponentially depend on work function and inversely depends upon the absolute temperature.

According to Richardson, the emission current density 'J' can be expressed as,

$$J = At^2 e^{(-\Phi/KT)} \text{ Ampers/m}^3$$

Where A-Emission constant $(A/m^3/K^2)$

Φ - Work function

T – absolute temperature (Kelvin)

K – Boltzman constant

J - emission current density.

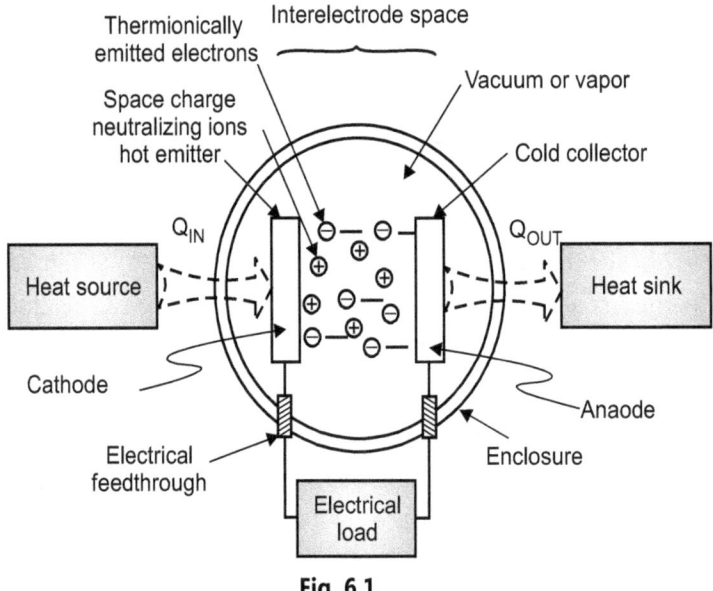

Fig. 6.1

Working

The electrons within a metal can be treated as "electron gas" in which individual outer most electrons are capable of moving freely under the influence of a field.

- This movement of electrons is responsible for the function of electric circuits. At the surface of a metal, a potential barrier exists which prevents the electrons from escaping. It is known from the free electron theory, at 0 K, all the energy levels up to E_F (fermi energy) are completely filled and all the energy level above the E_F are empty. The energy level from the surface of metallic cathode to the level of EF (BC in fig. 6.2) is the potential energy barrier called work function $(.\phi)$. If any electron wants to escape from the surface of the metallic cathode, they should cross this potential barrier.At 0K, all the electrons are bound within fermi energy level and cannot escape from the surface of cathode (emitter).When the thermal energy is supplied on the emitter side, some of the electrons are promoted to above the fermi level. These activated electrons can cross the potential energy barrier and escape from the surface of cathode and responsible for the current production. As long as the temperature is increased, the number of electrons escapes from the surface of emitter increases. Collector collects the emitted electrons and there is an external circuit through which the current flows. The thermionic emission current density is determined by the 'work function' of the material, which is basically the magnitude of the potential energy barrier. Good emitters should have low work functions.

- Thoriated tungsten is the best cathode metal because of its lower value of work function. It can be heated in two different ways.

    (a) Direct Heating : In the direct heating the filament itself is the cathode. Pure tungsten is used as main metal in the case of direct heating method.

    (b) Indirect Heating : In Indirect heating the cathode is heated by a separate filament. Nickel (or) Nickel alloys are used as main metal in the case of indirect heating.

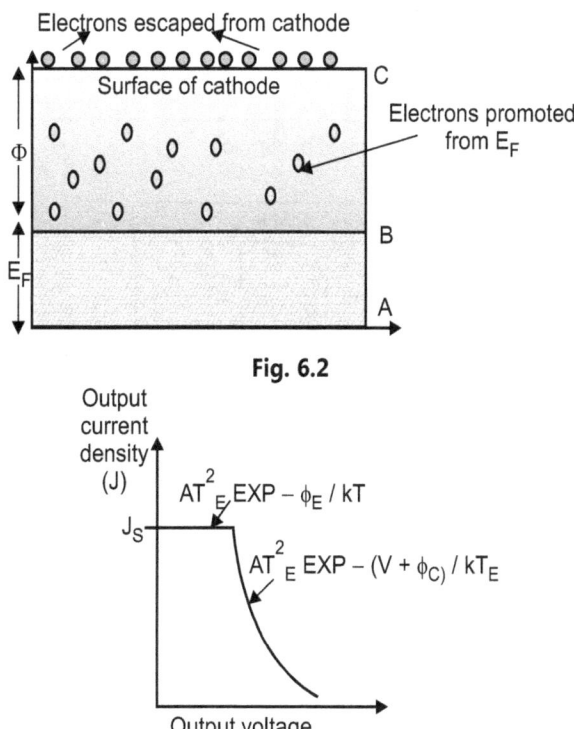

Fig. 6.2

Fig. 6.3 : Ideal thermionic diode characteristics.

Advantages of Thermionic Converter

- Rotating equipment is not employed.
- Separators for fluid not required
- Friction losses are not present.

Disadvantages of Thermionic Converter are

- Individual converter are low voltage, high current devices.
- Large number of converters must be sequentially arranged to obtain useful voltage.
- Power losses in leads can cut useful power.

Applications of Thermionic Converter

- They are used in space power application for spacecraft.

- They are used to power submarines and boats.

- They are used in water pump for irrigation,

- They are used in power plant for industry and domestic purpose

6.2   THERMOELECTRIC GENERATOR

Thermoelectric generators are also called Seebeck generators. These devices convert heat i.e.temperature differences directly into electrical energy, using a phenomenon called the Seebeck effect

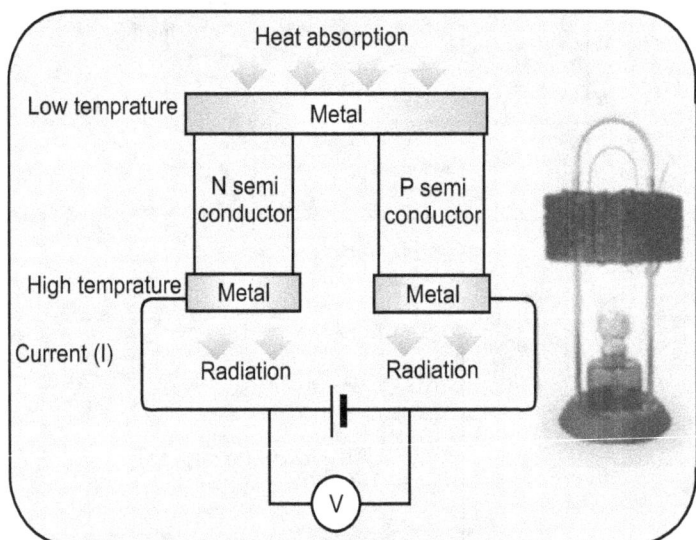

Fig. 6.4

The thermal-electrical conversion is done by a phenomenon generally referred to as "Seebeck effect". TEGs are solid-state device, which means that they have no moving parts during their operations. Together with features that they produce no noise and involve no harmful agents, they are the most widely adopted devices for waste heat recovery.

Seebeck Effect : Seebeck effect is the conversion of temperature differences directly into electricity. The conductor materials used to generate Seebeck effect are two different metals or semiconductors.

Seebeck coefficient of a material, is a measure of the magnitude of an induced thermoelectric voltage in response to a temperature difference across that material. The Seebeck coefficient has units of V/K, though it is more practical to use mV/K. The Seebeck coefficient of a material is represented by S or σ, and is non-linear as a function of temperature, and dependent on the conductors' absolute temperature, material and molecular structure.

Table 6.1 Seebeck Coefficients for Some Common Elements

Material	Seebeck Coeff.	Material	Seebeck Coeff.	Material	Seebeck Coeff.
Aluminum	3.5	Gold	6.5	Rhodium	6.0
Antimony	47	Iron	19	Selenium	900
Bismuth	-72	Lead	4.0	Silicon	440
Cadmium	7.5	Mercury	0.60	Silver	6.5
Carbon	3.0	Nichorme	25	Sodium	-2.0
Constantan	-35	Nickel	-15	Tantalum	4.5
Copper	6.5	Platinum	0	Tellurium	500
Germanium	300	Potassium	-9.0	Tungsten	7.5

As in fig. 6.4 the materials used in the two legs are n- and p-type semiconductors. If we denote their respective Seebeck coefficients to be Sn and Sp, the open circuit voltage Voc generated by this TE couple is then governed by the equation:

$$V_{OC} = \int_{T_c}^{T_h} (S_n(T) - S_p(T))\, dT$$

If the Seebeck coefficients are approximately constant for the measured temperature range in the TE legs then

$$V_{OC} = (S_n - S_p) \bullet (T_h - T_c).$$

If the temperature difference ΔT between the two ends of a material is small, then the Seebeck coefficient of this material is approximately defined as:

$$S = \frac{\Delta V}{\Delta T}$$

In a TEG where two ends of the n- and p-type legs are at different temperature levels, charge carriers in the leg material tend to diffuse in the direction which can help to reach thermodynamic equilibrium within the leg. Charge carriers originally at the end with higher temperature will move toward the cold side of TEG, and cold carriers move toward the hot side. If temperature difference is intentionally kept constant, the diffusion of charge carriers will form a constant heat current, hence a constant electrical current.

In fig. 6.4 the side with higher temperature, will drive electrons in the n-type leg toward the cold side, crossing the metallic interconnect, and pass into the p-type leg, thus creating a current through the circuit. Holes in the p-type leg will then follow in the direction of the current. The current can then be used to power a load.

If the rate of diffusion of hot and cold carriers were equal, there would be no net change in charge within the TE leg. Since scattering is energy-dependent, the hot and cold charge carriers will diffuse at different rates, which then create a potential difference, i.e. an electrostatic voltage, in the leg. This electric field, on the other hand, opposes the uneven scattering, and equilibrium will be finally reached given enough time. The thermopower of a material depends greatly on impurities, imperfections, and structural changes, with the latter affected often by temperature and electric field.

A phonon is a quantum mechanical description of a special type of vibrational motion, in which a lattice uniformly oscillates at the same frequency. Phonons are not always in local thermal equilibrium; they move against the thermal gradient. They lose momentum by interacting with electrons (or other carriers) and imperfections in the crystal. The phonon-electron scattering is predominant in phonon drag in a temperature region approximately defined by equation:

$$T \approx \frac{1}{5} \theta_D$$

where

θ_D is the Debye temperature.

This temperature is approximately around 200 K. At lower temperatures there are fewer phonons available for drag, and at higher temperatures they tend to lose momentum in phonon-phonon scattering instead of phonon-electron scattering.

Limitations of Thermoelectric Generator

- Low efficiency and high cost
- **High Output Resistance :** in order to get a significant output voltage a very high Seebeck coefficient is needed (high V/°C). A common approach is to place many thermo-elements in series, causing the effective output resistance of a generator to be very high (>10Ω). Thus power is only efficiently transferred to loads with high resistance; power is otherwise lost across the output resistance.
- **Adverse Thermal Characteristics :** because low thermal conductivity is required for a good thermoelectric generator, this can severely dampen the heat dissipation of such a device

6.3 MHD GENERATION

The word magneto hydro dynamics (MHD) is derived from magneto which means magnetic field, and hydro which means liquid, and dynamics meaning movement. The concept of MHD power generation was introduced for the very first time by Michael Faraday in the year 1832 in his Bakerian lecture to the Royal Society. He carried out an experiment at the Waterloo Bridge in Great Britain for measuring the current, from the flow of the river Thames in earth's magnetic field. This experiment outlined the basic concept behind MHD generation over the years .Later in August 13, 1940 this concept of magneto hydro dynamic power generation, was imbibed as the most widely accepted process for the conversion of heat energy directly into electrical energy without a mechanical sub-link.

As the name implies magneto hydro dynamics (MHD) is concerned with the flow of a conducting fluid in the presence of magnetic and electric field. The fluid may be gas at elevated temperatures or liquid metals like sodium or potassium. MHD generator is a device for converting heat energy of a fuel directly into electrical energy without conventional electric generator.

MHD converter system is a heat engine in which heat taken up at a higher temperature is partly converted into useful work and the remainder is rejected at a temperature. The thermal efficiency of MHD converter is increased by supplying the heat at the highest practical temperature and rejecting it at the lowest practical temperature. The output of the MHD is supplied to the conventional Plants. In advanced countries MHD generators are widely used but in developing countries like INDIA, it is still under construction.

Principle of MHD Power Generation

When an electric conductor moves across a magnetic field, a voltage is induced in it which produces an electric current. This is the principle of the conventional generator where the conductors consist of copper strips. The solid conductors are replaced by a gaseous conductor, an ionized gas in MHD generator. A pressurized, electrically conducting fluid flows through a transverse magnetic field in a channel or duct. Pair of electrodes are located on the channel walls at right angle to the magnetic field and connected through an external circuit to deliver power to a load connected to it. The MHD generator develops DC power and the conversion to AC is done using an inverter.

The induced EMF is given by

$$E = u \times B$$

where   u = velocity of the conductor.

B = magnetic field ointensity.

The induced current is given by,

$$I = C \times E$$

where   C = electric conductivity

6.3.1 Types of MHD Systems

MHD systems are classified into following types

- Open cycle system
- Closed cycle system
- Liquid metal system

Open Cycle System : The fuel (coal, oil or natural gas) is burnt in the combustor or combustion chamber. The compressed air is used to burn the coal in the combustion chamber to attain high temperatures. A lower preheat temperature would be adequate if the air is enriched in oxygen. The hot gases coming from combustor are seeded with a small amount of ionized alkali metal like cesium or potassium, to increase the electrical conductivity of the gas. Generally potassium carbonate which is seed material is injected into the combustion chamber. The gases coming out at high temperature after seeding is passed through MHD at a velocity of 700m/sec to 800 m/sec. The interaction between the flowing plasma and magnetic field produces electricity. For MHD system coupled with steam plants, this heat of the hot gases coming out from MHD can be used for steam generation before it is exhausted to atmosphere.

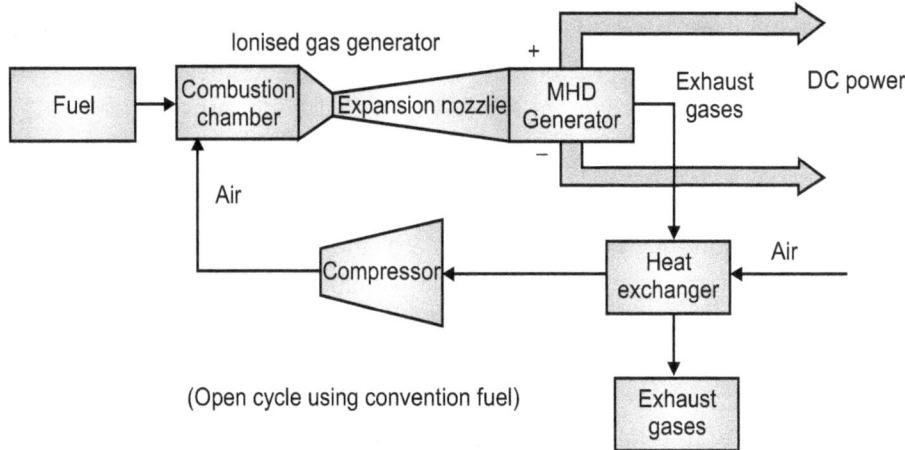

Fig. 6.5

The expansion nozzle reduces the gas pressure and consequently increases the plasma speed through the generator duct to increase the power output .The pressure drop causes the plasma temperature to fall which also increases the plasma resistance. The exhaust heat from the working fluid is used to drive a compressor to increase the fuel combustion rate but much of the heat will be wasted unless it can be used in another process.

Closed Cycle System : Closed cycle MHD system use rare gases as working fluid. The working fluid is continuously circulated in the cycle. Noble gases like helium, neon, argon, xenon, and krypton are most suitable. Helium is readily available as compared to neon so it is commonly used. With noble gases, calcium can be used as seed material instead of potassium. As there is no loss working fluid, this system has better heat transfer and electrical properties. Contrary to the open loop system there is no inlet and outlet for the atmospheric air.

Liquid Metal System : When a liquid metal with high electrical conductivity is used as working fluid, it is called a liquid metal MHD system. Main difficulty in these systems is the production of liquid flow with high kinetic energy from a thermal power source. Also this system has constructional and operational difficulties.

Advantages of MHD System

- These systems permit better fuel utilization.

- It has no moving parts, so more reliable.

- It is possible to use MHD for peak power generations and emergency service.

- The cost cannot be predicted very accurately, but capital costs of MHD plants will be competitive to oconventional steam plants. The overall operational costs in a plant would be about 20% less than conventional steam plants.

- Direct conversion of heat into electricity eliminates the turbine as compared with a gas turbine power plant. Also as compared with a steam power plant, both the boiler and the turbine elimination reduce loss of energy. The reduced fuel consumption offer additional economic benefits. It also leads to conservation of energy oresources.

- The closed cycle system produces power which is pollution free.

- Size of plant is smaller than conventional fossil fuel plants.

- MHD system has high thermal efficiency.

6.4 FUEL CELL

A fuel cell is an electrochemical device that combines hydrogen or other fuels and oxygen to produce electricity, with water and heat as its by-product. As long as fuel is supplied, the fuel cell will continue to generate power. Since the conversion of the fuel to energy takes place via an electrochemical process, the process is clean, quiet and highly efficient. In addition to low or zero emissions, benefits include high efficiency and reliability, multi-fuel capability, operation flexibility, durability, and ease of maintenance. Fuel cells are also scalable and can be stacked until the desired power output is reached. Since fuel cells operate silently, they reduce noise pollution as well as air pollution and the waste heat from a fuel cell can be used to provide hot water or space heating for a home or office.

Fuel cells are different from batteries in that they require a continuous source of fuel and oxygen/air to sustain the chemical reaction whereas in a battery the chemicals present in the battery react with each other to generate an emf. Fuel cells can produce electricity continuously for as long as these inputs are supplied.

The first fuel cells were invented in 1838. The first commercial use of fuel cells came more than a century later in NASA space programs to generate power for probes, satellites and space capsules. Since then, fuel cells have been used in many other applications. Fuel cells are used for primary and backup power for commercial, industrial and residential buildings and in remote or inaccessible areas. They are also used to power fuel-cell vehicles, including forklifts, automobiles, buses, airplanes, boats, motorcycles and submarines.

Construction and Working of Fuel Cell

For any type of fuel cell, there are mainly three segments.

- Anode
- Cathode
- Electrolyte

The type of electrolyte used is what defines the type of fuel cell used. Whatever may be the type of fuel cell, their basic operation is always the same.

With the combination of the three segments, two main chemical reactions take place. A catalyst will be present at the anode. This anode catalyst, mostly platinum powder, is used to oxidize the hydrogen fuel. Thus the hydrogen gas turns into ions and electrons. Out of these, the ions make way through the electrolyte to the cathode. As soon as they reach the cathode, they combine with the cathode and then react with the oxidant to produce water. The electrons pass through a wire producing the electricity. Nickel is mostly used as the cathode catalyst. Thus the electricity is formed at the load and water is obtained as the by-product.

Though a fuel cell can normally produce only up to 0.7 volts at full load, the desired amount of voltage can be obtained by combining the fuel cells in series. For obtaining the desired amount of current, the fuel cells can be connected in parallel.

The fuel cell also has certain losses which causes a lesser amount of voltage to be produced at a higher current rate. Some of the losses are ohmic loss. Activation loss and also the loss due to the mass depletion of reactants called mass transport loss.

Working of H_2-O_2 Fuel Cell

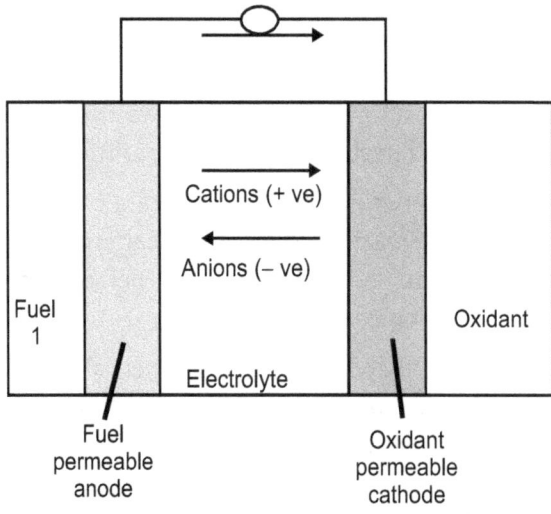

Fig. 6.6

The fuel is oxidized on the anode and oxidant reduced on the cathode. One species of ions are transported from one electrode to the other through the electrolyte to combine there with their counterparts, while electrons travel through the external circuit producing the electrical current.

The Fuel gas is passed towards the anode where the following oxidation reaction occurs

$$H_2 (g) = 2H+ + 2e-$$

The liberated electrons from hydrogen in anode side do not migrate through electrolyte.

They pass through the external circuit where work is performed, then finally goes into the cathode. On the other hand, the positive hydrogen ions (H+) migrate across the electrolyte towards the cathode.

At the cathode side the hydrogen atom reacts with oxygen gas (from air) and electrons to form water as byproduct. The cell reaction is

$$fuel + oxidant \longrightarrow product + Heat$$

$$H_2 + 1/2\ O_2 + 2e^- \longrightarrow H_2O + Heat$$

Advantages of Fuel Cells

- It is compact, light weight and has no moving parts. Thus it is 99.9% reliable.

- Fuel cells convert chemical energy directly into electricity without the combustion process. As a result, Fuel cells can achieve high efficiencies in energy conversion.

- Pollution is reduced by 99%. This is the lowest pollution rate when compared to batteries as well as gasoline powered devices.

- A high power density allows fuel cells to be relatively compact source of electric power, beneficial in application with space constraints.

- Fuel cells can be used in residential or built-up areas where the noise pollution can be avoided.

Disadvantages of Fuel Cells

- The anode catalysts like platinum and also gas diffusion layers almost hold up to 75% of the total cost. When compared to batteries and gasoline powered vehicles, they tend to be the costliest. The overall production cost of a fuel cell is very costly.

- Most of the fuel cells that are used in cars, like PEMFC does not operate well enough in higher temperatures. As a result they have less tolerance level and less stability under running conditions.

- In order to make vehicles with fuel cells enough amount of hydrogen has to be generated. After generation process, they must also be carefully transported from the generating plants. This can be done only by transportation or pipelines. For this a proper infrastructure has not yet been developed.

6.5   SOLAR CELLS

The basic ingredients of solar cells are semiconductor materials, such as silicon. For solar cells, a thin semiconductor wafer creates an electric field, on one side positive and negative on the other. When light energy hits the solar cell, electrons are knocked loose from the atoms in the semiconductor material. When electrical conductors are connected to the positive and negative sides an electrical circuit is formed and electrons are captured in the form of an electric current that is, electricity. This electricity is used to power a load. A PV cell can either be circular or square in construction.

Photovoltaic (PV) cells are made up of at least 2 semi-conductor layers. One layer containing a positive charge,and the other a negative charge. As a PV cell is exposed to sunlight, many of the photons are reflected, pass right through, or absorbed by the solar cell. When enough photons are absorbed by the negative layer of the photovoltaic cell, electrons are freed from the negative semiconductor material. Due to the manufacturing process of the positive layer, these freed electrons naturally migrate to the positive layer creating a voltage differential, similar to a household battery.When the 2 layers are connected to an external load, the electrons flow through the circuit creating electricity. Each individual solar energy cell produces only 1-2 watts. To increase power output, cells are combined in a weather-tight package called a solar module. These modules are then wired up in serial and/or parallel with one another, into what's called a solar array, to create the desired voltage and amperage output required by the given project.

Mathematical modeling of photovoltaic module is describe below

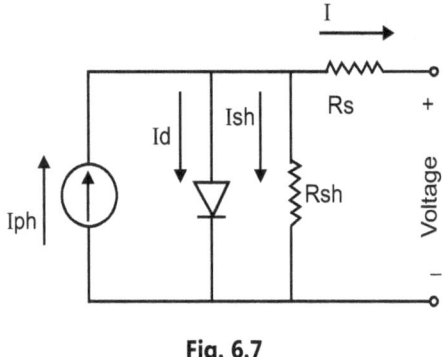

Fig. 6.7

I_{ph} : Photocurrent;

I_d : Current through parallel diode;

I_{sh}: Shunt current;

I : Output current;

V : Output voltage;

D : Parallel diode;

R_{sh} : Shunt resistance;

R_s : Series resistance

The basic equation from the theory of semiconductors that mathematically describes the I–V characteristic of the ideal PV cell is

$$I = I_{ph} - I_0 \left\{ e^{\frac{q(V+R_sI)}{AKT}} - 1 \right\} - \frac{V + R_sI}{R_{sh}} \tag{1}$$

Where,

I_0 is the reverse saturation current of the diode,

q is the electron charge (1.602×10^{-19} C),

A is the curve fitting factor,

K is Boltzmann constant (1.38×10^{-23} J/K)

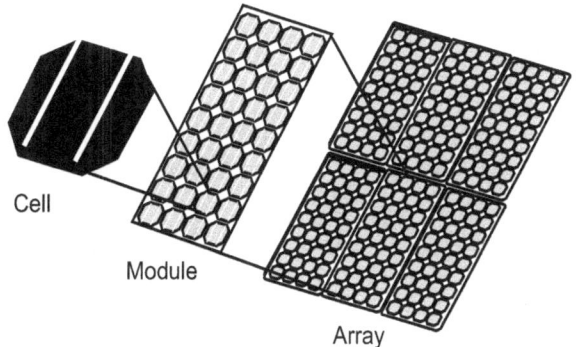

Fig. 6.8

QUESTIONS

1. Explain the Thermionic converter.

2. Define Thermionic effect?

3. State the law of Richardson.

4. Discuss the Advantages, Disadvantages and Applications of Themionic Converter.

5. Describe the Thermoelectric Generator.

6. Write a short note on fuel cell.

7. Explain the solar cell.

8. Explain the MHD generation and describe the principle of MHD power generation.

9. Write a short note of types of MHD systems.

10. What are the advantages of MHD systems ?

✠ ✠ ✠